AWO

BIG TIME PLAYERS:

Episode Three - Card Subject To Change

Written By Emerson A. Cotton

Be Sure to Read AWO Big Time Players: Episode One - The Beginning of Change and AWO Big Time Players - Episode Two: Continuing to Grow <u>Before</u> Diving Into This Episode.

Prologue:

Description of Visual: *We begin with a black screen.*
Suddenly,

**THE FOLLOWING
WAS RECORDED
WHEN EPISODE TWO
WENT OFF THE AIR**

Appears on the screen in white letters.
*As the words fade away, we hear "The Rock Star" Joey Adams lay down an
ominous warning.*

"The Rock Star" Joey Adams: Dale… you can run for now! But I promise
you, I'll make you pay for this!

Description of Visual: *The arena is still buzzing from Dale Garvin's action.
As we fade in, we see the back of Natasha Moore. She's backstage, with a
microphone in hand. She appears to be in hot pursuit of something, or someone.*

Natasha Moore: Come on! I think he's heading for the back door!

Description of Visual: *The cameraman continues to follow Natasha as she
anxiously looks around.*
Suddenly, something catches her attention.

Natasha Moore: There he is!

Description of Visual: *Natasha increases her speed as she tries to catch "The
Natural" Dale Garvin, who is about to head out the backdoor.*

Natasha Moore: Dale! Dale! Just a quick question!

Description of Visual: *Natasha and the cameraman, close in on Dale. Dale
gets exasperated and quickly shuts Natasha down.*

"The Natural" Dale Garvin: Look! I know what you're about to ask! What
happened out there was an accident! A happy accident! But an accident
nonetheless!
So am I sorry?
Not at all!
And you tell Joey, when I see *him*, I'm gonna…

Description of Visual: *Dale cuts off his words when he sees someone.*
approaching.

"The Natural" Dale Garvin: I don't have time for this, pal! I'm outta here!

Description of Visual: *As Dale begins to step out the door, we here Jack*
Houston call out to him.

Jack Houston: You just hang on there, Dale, cause you're going to want to hear
this!

Description of Visual: *Dale rolls his eyes and waits as Jack storms into the*
scene.

Jack Houston: Listen, I don't want to see you here next week! In fact, don't
come back until I call for you!

Description of Visual: *Dale looks stunned.*

"The Natural" Dale Garvin: What about my match?

Jack Houston: You'll get your match, when I say so and how I say so!

Description of Visual: *Dale aggressively opens the door.*
He looks back at Jack and says one more thing.

"The Natural" Dale Garvin: You know what Jack? I'll stay home! But you
better not screw me out of what's mine!

Description of Visual: *Dale forces the door off his shoulder.*
He aggressively leaves the building.
As Jack tries to regain his composure, Natasha looks at Jack, and asks him a
question.

Natasha Moore: So what now?

Description of Visual: *Jack takes a deep a breath and responds.*

Jack Houston: I need to go talk to Joey.

Natasha Moore: Should we come with you?

Description of Visual: *Jack nods.*

Jack Houston: Yeah. Come on.

Description of Visual: *We follow Jack and Natasha as they walk through the hallway. There are lots of people around, buzzing over Dale's actions.
We can't quite make out what he is saying, but we can hear Jack muttering to himself, every step of the way.
Natasha gives Jack a look of concern.*

Natasha Moore: Are you okay, Jack?

Jack Houston: I will be.
I've got some big plans for the upcoming weeks and I got a ton of things to take care of.
Plus I've got to deal with this and…

Description of Visual: *Jack lets out a big sigh.*

Natasha Moore: Running a wrestling company isn't easy is it?

Jack Houston: No it is not.
Do you know anyone that would want to be my assistant?

Natasha Moore: Uh…not right off hand. But I'll let you know.

Description of Visual: *Jack and Natasha reach the trainer's room and walk through the door. Inside they find Joey, pacing frantically, with his hands to his head.*

Jack Houston: Joey?

Description of Visual: *Joey is oblivious to both Jack and Natasha.*

Jack Houston: Joey!

Description of Visual: *Joey snaps to and looks at Jack. He tries to hold it *together but there is great concern in his eyes.*

"The Rock Star" Joey Adams: H-hey Jack.

Jack Houston: How's Lola?

Description of Visual: *It gets harder for Joey to hold it together.*

"The Rock Star" Joey Adams: Sh…she's…in the back getting checked out.

Description of Visual: *Joey's expression changes. Multiple emotions well up inside of him, and they all appear on Joey's face.*

"The Rock Star" Joey Adams: Her face, Jack!
He hit her in the face!

Description of Visual: *Jack pats Joey on the shoulder.*

Jack Houston: Listen, I just wanted to let you know that I told Dale not to show up next week. So I'm asking you to please do the same.

Description of Visual: *Jack's words confused and upset Joey.*

"The Rock Star" Joey Adams: Are you suspending us? You can't do that! I have to get my hands Dale!

Description of Visual: *Jack can tell that Joey is becoming frantic, and quickly interjects.*

Jack Houston: No. I'm not suspending you or Dale.
But as personal as things have just gotten between you two, I know I won't be able to keep you two apart next week.
Next week is going to be the start of some big things and I can't focus on keeping you two apart and running the show.
So, please… stay home. Try to cool off. And I'll try to decide what type of match you two are going have, the week after next.

"The Rock Star" Joey Adams: Jack I…

Jack Houston: Please Joey. For me. I promise, I will have a match decided and announced, by the end of next week's show.

Description of Visual: *Joey runs his hands down his face, as he lets out a heavy sigh.*

"The Rock Star" Joey Adams: Jack, out of respect for you, I'll stay home. But when me and Dale have our rematch, it doesn't matter what type of match it is, dude, I'm going to be *very* disrespectful.

Description of Visual: *Jack let's out a sigh of relief.*

Jack Houston: Thank you Joey.
I'll leave you be.

Description of Visual: *Jack starts to walk away, but stops in mid-stride.*
He places his hand on Joey's shoulder.

Jack Houston: And don't worry. As they say back home, Lola's a tough ol' gal. It's gonna take more than a punch to keep her down.

Description of Visual: *A smile appears on Joey's face as he looks at Jack.*

"The Rock Star" Joey Adams: Thanks Jack.
You're right. She is tough.

Description of Visual: *Jack gives Joey a nod of approval, before leaving the room.*
As he closes the door, he closes his eyes and exhales heavily.

Jack Houston: Guess I've got some restructuring to do for next week.

Fade to Black

Scene Change

Description of Visual: *As we fade in on our shot, the Word* LIVE *appears in the lower right hand corner of the screen.*
We begin to see Eric Wesley, our play-by-play announcer, and the musclebound, legendary wrestler, Super Stud Marcus Ryan, our color commentator.
After Super Stud shows off his, yellow **Stud 24/7** *shirt, Eric adjust his black framed glasses, and greets us, the viewing audience.*

Eric Wesley: Hello everyone and welcome to another edition of AWO Big Time players.
Thanks you for joining us.
We've got a great show lined up for you all.
Unfortunately, I have to deliver some bad news.
If you all remember, at the end of last week's episode, it was announced by AWO President, Jack Houston, that Lola was going to receive a shot at the AWO Women's Championship tonight.

Super Stud: A championship by the way, held by "The Sexy Lioness" Tamara Starbuck!

Eric: Well Unfortunately, because of Dale's actions last week…

Super Stud: Dale's *unintentional* actions

Eric: *[Sighs]* …Lola now has a concussion, a broken nose, and a fractured orbital bone. Because of this, Lola was not cleared for competition and will be out of action for several weeks.
Now, there will be a replacement match tonight and that match will be between two of the top contenders, in the women's division: "The Sensational" Angel Young, and Lethal E. The winner of the match, will receive, what's being called a "special" opportunity.

Super Stud: Special opportunity? What does that mean?

Eric: I believe Jack's going to make that announcement later tonight.
I've also been told that later in the evening, the help of the AWO audience will be needed.

Super Stud: What type of help can they give?

Eric: All I was told was that it pertains to the Modern Marvel tournament and that the people need to be prepared, to make their voices heard.

Super Stud: Oh when have their voices ever mattered?

Eric: Anyway… in the final match of the night, there will be a tag team match. Hagan Benally and Evan Skaggs - The Sixth Street Soldiers, with Cali Ivy in their corner, will be taking on Joseph Seone and Jacob Leone - The Titans of Tomorrow. The winner of the tag match will take on Trueno and Racha, Los

Intensa Tormenta, next week. *And* the winner of *that* match, will get a shot at the AWO World Tag Team champions, "Classy" Billy Foxx and The Jigga-Man Jamal Ryans.

Super Stud: The tag division is heating up here in the AWO!

Eric: Yes it is!
Oh, I almost forgot: Next week, "The Rock Star" Joey Adams and "The Natural" Dale Garvin will face each other in a rematch for the AWO World Championship. And at the end of the night, Jack Houston is going to announce what type of match they will be having.

Super Stud: It could be a first blood match! Or it could be a last man standing match! Oh! Maybe it's a submission match?

Eric: It could be any of those three matches or it could be something else. We'll have to wait and see.
Right now folks, our opening contest is going to be a rematch for the AWO *New Age* Championship. The newcomer to the AWO, Sonny Simpson Jr. will take on the AWO New Age Champion, "The Exceptional" Mark Sandal. And people are expecting those two to tear the house down!
It really is, going to be a great night, jam packed with action!
But, before we get into it, it's time to hear the rules of combat.

Rules of Combat:

* The object of a standard match is to force your opponent's shoulders to the mat for the referee's count of three. A three-count takes place when the referee hits the mat three times in succession.
* Victory can also happen by forcing your opponent to submit, typically with the use of a submission hold. A combatant can signal that he submits in two ways: If he or she verbally says, "I quit" or by rapidly tapping the mat, which is called "tapping out" to his opponent.
* If a combatant reaches the ropes with any part of their body, it will force a pin-fall count to cease or a submission hold to be broken.
* In the event of a submission hold needing to be broken, the combatant administering the hold will have a count of five to release their opponent. They will risk a disqualification, if they do not release their opponent by five.
* A wrestler cannot choke the air from an opponent, punch with a closed fist or pull an opponent's hair.

* If an illegal chokehold is applied, the one applying the hold will have a referee's count of five to break the hold.
* Pulling the hair or using a closed fist will result in a verbal warning the first time it occurs. The wrestler will be disqualified if it happens again. Use of a weapon will result in an instant disqualification.
* Weapons cannot be used at anytime during the match. Use of a weapon will result in an instant disqualification.
* Outside parties (i.e. managers, friends of the combatants or another wrestler) are not permitted to enter into the match. If an outside party does enter into a match and attacks one of the combatants, the combatant who was not attacked will be disqualified.
* The match must remain in the confines of the 20-foot-by 20-foot ring at all times. If one or both combatants leave the ring for any reason, the combatant or combatants will have until the referee's count of ten to get back into the ring or they will lose the match via count out.
* If both combatants are knocked down in the ring at the same time, one or both opponents will have until the referee's count of ten to get back to their feet. Once at least one person is standing, the match will continue.
* In a title match, the title can only change hands by a pin-fall or submission. If a count-out or disqualification occurs, the champion retains his or her championship.
* During a tag team match- teams of two or more wrestlers, competing against each other-only one "legal" person is allowed in the ring at all times. To be declared legal, a person's partner has to tag him or her into the match. The referee will either reprimand or disqualify the team, if an illegal person stays in the ring for a referee's count of five.
* The referee is not allowed to be harmed in any way. If one of the competitors does harm the referee, the offender will be instantly disqualified.
* In special cases, a match may not conform to these rules. In those cases a unique set of rule will be in place.

Super Stud: So folks, with all that out of the way, get ready to experience pro wrestling at its finest.

The Beginning

Description of Visual: *A series of pyrotechnics explode at the staging area, both scaring and exciting the audience. This explosive display means that the action is about to begin.*
We pan over to a shot of the ring, where we find our ring announcer, Tony

Anderson. Tony has his microphone in hand, and is ready to introduce the competitors of the first match.

Tony Anderson: Ladies and gentlemen, our opening contest, is scheduled for one-fall, and is for the AWO New Age Championship.

Description of Visual: *The fans begin cheering wildly with anticipation of this rematch.*
An upbeat hip-hop instrumental, begins playing throughout the arena. Since the fans are now a little more familiar with the challenger, they start to cheer when they hear his music.

Tony Anderson: Introducing first, the challenger: He hails from Baltimore, Maryland and weighs in at two-hundred and twenty-five pounds. His name is, Sonny…Simpson…Jr.

Description of Visual: *We see a shot of the fans as they continue to cheering, anticipating Sonny's arrival.*

Eric: Sonny has really garnered a lot of support since his debut.

Super Stud: Well we'll find out if what happened in his debut, was just a fluke.

Description of Visual: *We cut to a shot of the stage, just in time to see Sonny walk out.*
As we watch Sonny making his way to the ring, we see that he is wearing a black jacket zipped halfway up, a pair of slightly baggy red pants, that are tucked into a pair of mid-cut white boots.

Eric: There he is Eric! The man some people feel *should* be the New Age Champion!

Super Stud: He probably *would* be champ, if he had gotten his shoulder off the mat.

Eric: Well, you of all people know that its hard to be in the right frame of mind after competing for a long period of time.

Super Stud: Are you really trying to tell me about a competitor's frame of mind?

Eric: No. Just making conversation.
You know people don't just pay for the matches, they pay for our witty banter as well.

Super Stud: Witty banter? Who says that anymore?

Eric: I do.
Speaking of me saying things, I want to say that I was so excited in the first episode, that I don't think I properly explained the significance of the AWO New Age Championship.

Super Stud: Wow! You actually made a mistake?

Eric: Your sarcasm isn't lost on me.
Anyway, the reason that the New Age Championship is so important, is because it's the secondary title, or a gateway title if you will. As long as a wrestler is holding the New Age Championship, he can challenge for the AWO World Championship at any time. Not only that, but until you win the New Age Championship, you can not even THINK about challenging for the World Championship.

Super Stud: So basically what you're saying is, unless you're either the holder of the New Age Championship or a *former* holder of the New Age Championship, you won't even be considered for an AWO World Championship title match?

Eric: Exactly.

Super Stud: Oh.
Well why didn't you just say that?

Eric: I…I don't know.

Super Stud: Well hopefully you'll do better in the future.

Description of Visual: *The thing that really stands out about Sonny, is that he has a big smile on his face. A smile that is primarily because he appreciates the second opportunity he is being given and the reception he is receiving from the fans.*

Super Stud: Do you think he's going to smile like that if he *doesn't* win the title tonight?

Eric: Well he was smiling when Natasha Moore caught up with him earlier. So let's show everyone that footage right now.

Scene Change:

Description of Visual: *We transition to a shot backstage. In the lower left hand corner of the screen, we see the words,* MOMENTS AGO.
Sonny is standing in front of a locker room door with the lovely, blonde haired backstage corespondent, Natasha Moore.
Natasha has a microphone in hand and is prepared to talk to the challenger.

Natasha Moore: I'm here with Sonny Simpson Jr. who will be taking on "The Exceptional One" Mark Sandal. Sonny, you're getting a chance at redemption. Please tell us, what's going through your mind right now?

Description of Visual: *Sonny is so excited that he claps his hands and pumps his fists.*

Sonny Simpson Jr.: I can't believe this is happening! I'm actually getting a *second* chance at the New Age Championship!
Now the first one, didn't go the way I expected. But tonight, I plan on doing a lot better. I've talk with my dad and studied footage from the last match, so I know what I have to do. I know what mistakes I made and I'm not going to make them again. So Mark, you better be ready, cause if you thought I brought the fight before, I'm really going to bring it this time!

Description of Visual: *Still wearing a look of excitement, Sonny puts his hands on his hips and looks at Natasha. Natasha looks at him and nods before closing out the interview.*

Natasha: Okay. Thank you Sonny.

Scene Change

Description of Visual: *We return to the present, where we see Sonny in the ring, removing his jacket.*

Super Stud: Did he say he talked to his dad?

Eric: He's close to his dad. You know his dad was the one who trained him, right?

Super Stud: I know that. And I know his dad. But it still sounds dorky to me. And he's still wearing those suspenders.

Eric: Are you really that anti-suspenders?

Super Stud: Only nerds and geeks wear suspenders, Eric.

Description of Visual: *Sonny begins to stretch and loosen up before the match. At the same time, an alternative rock style instrumental, begins playing.*

Tony Anderson: His opponent is from Chicago, Illinois and weighs two-hundred and seventeen pounds. He is the current, reigning and defending, AWO New Age Champion. He is, "The Exceptional One," Mark Sandal.

Description of Visual: *The fans rise to their feet with excitement as they anticipate Mark's arrival.*

Eric: Listen to that ovation! You can't tell me the people don't love this guy!

Super Stud: That word love is serious thing.

Eric: What now?

Super Stud: Don't worry about it. It was from a song and it popped in my head!

Description of Visual: *Mark excitedly walks out onto the stage and raises his fists in the air. With the AWO New Age title around his waist, a pair of green tights with a blue psychedelic designs, and a pair of green and blue kick pads, over his black wrestling shoes, Mark makes his way to the ring.*
There's a smile on Mark's face as well. A smile that is primarily based off of the reaction he is receiving. Because of that reaction, Mark points to everyone in the arena, to show his appreciation.

Super Stud: Mark better stop pointing and get focused on this match! He didn't fair too well the last time they met!

Eric: Well he also had some things to say earlier about this match. And we're going to see those comments, right now.

Scene Change

Description of Visual: MOMENTS EARLIER *is once again in the lower left hand corner of the screen. Once again, we are backstage, with a different backstage corespondent, Lawrence Michaels.,Lawrence is standing next to "The Exceptional" Mark Sandal.*
There is a smile on Mark's face as he bounces side to side on the balls of his feet.

Lawrence Michaels: Mark Sandal, in a few moments, you will be defending the AWO New Age championship, against Sonny Simpson Jr. Based off of how things played out for you the last time you guys faced each other, what's going through your mind?

Description of Visual: *Mark adjust the title around his waist.and looks at Lawrence.*

Mark Sandal: What's going through my mind? The fact that I've held this title for a while now. The fact that I've defended it proudly against some great competitors. The fact that two weeks ago… I almost lost it.

Description of Visual: *Mark closes his eyes and takes a deep breath.*

Mark Sandal: You know that *almost* lose, has eaten at me since it happened. But luckily, Jack Houston, is giving both Sonny and I, a shot at redemption. Sonny you really pushed me to my limits. And I'm really looking forward to going at it with you one more time. But this time, I'm taking it…to a whole new level.

Description of Visual: *Mark starts to walk away. He stops, turns towards us and has a serious expression on his face.*

Mark Sandal: Before I leave, I want to say something to Payne.
Payne, I know you're next in line for a shot at *my* New Age title. I know *exactly* what you're capable of! And I know just how *dangerous* you can be!
But don't underestimate me either!
Anytime you want me, I'll be ready and waiting!

Description of Visual: *Mark intensely stares into the camera as we transition back to the arena.*

Scene Change:

Description of Visual: *We are once again live, where we see Mark climbing into the ring.*

Eric: Mark really sounded confident in that interview, Stud.

Super Stud: He did. But let's see if that confidence will carry over to a win?

Description of Visual: *Mark takes off his belt as he walks to the center of the ring.*
He raises the title belt in the air, for all the world to see.

Super Stud: He could be raising that championship belt above his head, for the last time.

Eric: You could be right, Stud.

Description of Visual: *We see Sonny in the corner, with his eyes locked on Mark.*
Sonny smiles and appears to be feeling confident, that the championship would soon be his.

Super Stud: Sonny keeping his eyes on the prize as they say.

Eric: You can't cross the finish line, if you can't see it.

Super Stud: What fortune cookie did you get that out of?

Description of Visual: *Mark hands the belt over to the official.*
As the official takes the belt, Mark moves backwards to his corner, rubbing his hands together and focusing on Sonny.
Meanwhile, Sonny begins bouncing side to side on his toes, getting himself loose and ready for the match.

Eric: Both of these men are ready for battle.

Super Stud: And everyone is ready to see this battle.

Description of Visual: *The referee walks to the center of the ring. He lifts the title belt above his head, signifying that the title is on the line in this match.*

Eric: And this match is about to get under…

Description of Audio: *Eric unexpectedly stops speaking.*

Super Stud: Under what, Eric?

Eric: Hold on.
I'm being told in my headset, that we need to wait a minute.

Description of Visual: *Just before the referee signals to the timekeeper to ring the bell, Tony Anderson raises his hand and signals for them to wait.*

Super Stud: What is going on?

Eric: I think we're about to find out.

Description of Visual: *Tony has his hand up to his earpiece and appears to be receiving a message.*
Once that message is received, Tony Anderson begins to make an announcement.

Tony Anderson: Ladies and gentlemen, I've been asked that you all welcome to the commentator's table, "The Swiss Aristocrat" Noah Peyrot.

Description of Visual: *As a chorus of boos fills the arena, we pan to the stage. Strolling out is the six feet, five inch tall, 232 pound, Noah Peyrot.*

Super Stud: This guy is going to join us? That's great! What a pleasant surprise! And look at that outfit he has on!

Description of Visual: *The outfit that Noah is wearing, is a black tapestry Victorian Aristocrat Vest over a blue button-up shirt. He also has on a pair of black Medieval pants and a pair of shiny black shoes. And in his left hand, he is carrying a black walking stick, with a brass top.*
Noah has the same arrogant demeanor as he had the previous week. What is different, is that this week, he is not alone.

Super Stud: Hey Eric, since you're always getting told stuff in your headset, any word on who Noah's friend is?

Eric: Nope. No word at all on who he is.

Description of Visual: *To Noah's right, clapping proudly is a bald, brown skinned man in a very expensive black business suit.*

Super Stud: Who ever that guy is, he seems really supportive of Noah.

Description of Visual: *We cut back to a shot of the ring, where we see Sonny and Mark watching Noah and his associate heading to ringside.*
Both Sonny and Mark appear to be confused about what's going on. They question the referee, who just tries to keep them calm and focused on the upcoming match. The live audience can not hear this, but we at home can hear the referee say, "once Noah and that other gentleman get seated, we'll get started."

Eric: I guess we're waiting for these two, because the referee doesn't want any distractions.

Super Stud: Just be patient, Eric. Greatness takes time.

Eric: .Now who sounds like a fortune cookie?

Description of Visual: *As Noah and his friend reach the commentator's table, Eric and Super Stud stand to greet them.*
Eric extends his hand, but Noah looks at him with disdain.

Super Stud: What's wrong with you? You don't shake hands with a man of his caliber.

Eric: I see.

Description of Visual: *As one ringside technician prepares a third headset, another ringside technician brings over a chair.*
Noah's friend aggressively takes the chair and slides it into place next to Stud.
Before Noah can sit, his friend pulls out a white cloth, and dusts off the chair.

Eric: Is this really necessary?

Super Stud: Yes Eric! This man is an aristocrat!
Actually, he's THE Aristocrat!
The Swiss Aristocrat.

Description of Visual: *Noah's friend motions for Noah to take a seat, prompting Noah to stroll over to his chair.*

Eric: Wow. This is uh…quite the presentation.

Super Stud: Have some patients Eric! And respect!

Description of Visual: *As Noah finally takes his seat, he slides into position and his friend quickly grabs the third headset.*

Eric: What is going on, now?

Super Stud: Just be quiet, Eric! Let them do what they need to do.

Description of Visual: *Noah's associate pulls a small spray bottle of sanitizing solution from inside of his jacket pocket, and sprays the headset.*

Eric: This is…this is a bit much.

Super Stud: You don't want the man to get ear fungus do you?

Eric: Ear fungus?

Super Stud: Shuh! Be quiet!

Description of Visual: *Noah's friend quickly puts the bottle back into his pocket. He reaches into his other pocket and pulls out another white cloth. He then proceeds to wipe down the headset.*

Eric: This guy is like a magician or something.

Super Stud: The man is just prepared, Eric. He was probably a…a boy scout or something.

Description of Visual: *Once the mysterious associate feels satisfied, he hands the headset to Noah and steps behind him.*

Super Stud: Guess he got out the gunk and whatnot.

Eric: Yeah. No need for Noah to worry about…ear fungus.

Description of Visual: *Noah place the headset on. As he adjust them, Eric and Super Stud are finally able to take their seats.*

"The Swiss Aristocrat" Noah Peyrot: Are you able to hear me gentlemen?

Super Stud: We can. And welcome sir.

Eric: Yes Noah, welcome.

Noah: If you please, I ask that you refer to me as "Mr. Peyrot."

Eric: Fair enough.
Mr. Peyrot, would you like to tell us who your friend is?

Noah: This is my associate, Lord Manny Hayes.

Eric: Lord? This man is a Lord?

Noah: Indeed. He also helps me with my day-to-day affairs.

Super Stud: That's amazing! You have a *lord* handling your day-to-day affairs!

"The Swiss Aristocrat" Noah: Yes I do!
Well, perhaps I should retract my statement. Manny isn't an *actual* "Lord," in the traditional sense of the word. Who he is, is a man who has helped me discover my roots and has become my personal assistant, as well as my most trusted adviser and confidant. As far as I am concerned, he is a lord amongst men. Hence why I refer to him as "Lord" Manny.

Eric: He sounds like a delightful person.

"The Swiss Aristocrat" Noah: Oh indeed he is.
That is why from this day forward, he will be accompanying me to the ring.

Super Stud: Oh that's wonderful!

I wish I had a friend like that I could trust.

Description of Visual: *We return our attention to the ring where Sonny and Mark have been watching both Noah and Lord Manny, in disbelief.*

"The Swiss Aristocrat" Noah: I must say, I do not understand why those two…competitors are observing me.

Super Stud: Probably your…dapper demeanor.

Noah: Perhaps you are correct. I am quite…dapper.

Eric: [*mumbled*] It's going to be a long night.

Noah: Beg your pardon, Eric?

Eric: Oh nothing. We should probably get ready to call the match.

Description of Visual: *Both Sonny and Mark return their focus to each other. They look at one another with expressions of confusion. Despite not being able to figure out Noah's intentions, Sonny and Mark once again get their heads back in the game.*

Eric: Well barring any interruptions, I think we're about to finally, get this match underway.

Description of Visual: *The referee ask Sonny if he is ready.*
Sonny nods.
The referee ask if Mark is ready.
Mark nods.
The referee signals for the time keeper to ring the bell.
With that, the match begins.

<u>**AWO New Age Championship Match: Challenger: Sonny Simpson Jr. Vs. Champion: "The Exceptional One" Mark Sandal**</u>

Description of Visual: *Both Sonny and Mark head to the center of the ring.*
Mark extends his fist to Sonny.
Sonny is unsure of Mark's intentions.

Super Stud: Sonny better be careful.

Eric: Really?
I think he can trust him.

Super Stud: We'll see.

Description of Visual: *Despite his uncertainty, Sonny raises his own fist to Mark.*
To everyone's surprise and relief, the two men touch fist in the middle of the ring.

Eric: Great show of sportsmanship by these two gentlemen.

"The Swiss Aristocrat" Noah Peyrot: I believe that it is clear, that these men aren't gentlemen.

Eric: Why do you say that?

Noah: Isn't it obvious? Gentlemen shake hands. Gentlemen don't…fist bump each other.
It is so uncultured.

Super Stud: He's right ya know?

Eric: Well you didn't shake my hand, Mr. Peyrot.

Super Stud: Probably because he doesn't know where your hand has been!

Noah: Exactly!

Description of Visual: *Sonny and Mark look like they are going to start off the match with a collar and elbow tie up.*
Before they can engage, Mark quickly slips behind Sonny and grabs him around the waist.

Eric: Mark starting things off, with a quick go-behind into a waist lock!

Description of Visual: *Before Sonny can react, Mark quickly moves next to Sonny, and tightly wraps his arms around Sonny's head.*

Eric: Mark now transitioning from a waist lock, to a headlock!

Description of Visual: *While Sonny is trying to formulate a counter, Mark once again goes back behind Sonny, and traps him in a waist lock.*

Super Stud: I have to give Mark credit, this appears to be a decent strategy. It keeps Sonny guessing and takes him off his game.

Description of Visual: *Mark quickly lifts Sonny up.*
He falls backwards, and drops Sonny shoulders, neck and upper back, onto the mat.

Eric: And Mark using a bridging German suplex! The same move that Sonny used on Mark!

Super Stud: Yeah! But unlike Sonny, Mark has his shoulders off the mat!

Description of Visual: *The referee quickly gets into position and checks Sonny's shoulders.*
The referee strikes the mat with his palm once. He strikes it a second time. But after some intense struggling, Sonny is able to get free before the three.

Eric: That was a two-count!

Super Stud: But it was almost a three!

Description of Visual: *Mark quickly gets to his feet.*
Sonny gets up afterwards.
Mark sees that Sonny is shook up and off balance and quickly moves close to him. He leaps into the air and drives both of his feet into Sonny's jaw.

Eric: And a beautiful dropkick by Mark, puts Sonny on the mat!

Description of Visual: *A shot of Sonny's face is caught on camera. He appears to be losing control and rolls out of the ring to the floor.*

Super Stud: I don't think this match is starting off, the way Sonny envisioned.

Description of Visual: *Sonny's anger gets the best of him. He turns around and kicks the barricades at ringside.*

Eric: Sonny losing his temper!

Super Stud: He better get it together and stop taking it out on our barricades cause here comes Mark!

Description of Visual: *Sonny turns back towards the ring.*
Sonny has no time to react. Mark flips over the top rope and lands, in a seated position, onto his chest.

Eric: And Mark taking Sonny off his feet with a flipping seated senton!

Super Stud: I have no idea how he does moves like that! But I do know, that Mark needs to keep it up! Sonny can't win if Sonny can't get focused!

Description of Visual: *Mark gets back to his feet and takes a minute to catch his breath. The fans jump to their feet and cheer at this exciting wrestling action.*

"The Swiss Aristocrat" Noah Peyrot: Stud, I must say that I am inclined to agree with what you said. But if I may, I'm not really impressed with this "wrestling" action.

Super Stud: Why is that?

"The Swiss Aristocrat" Noah Peyrot: Well Mark certainly is a tremendous athlete, to be sure. But, there's an old saying I once heard, any monkey can jump out of a tree.

Super Stud: Well said. You do have a point.

Eric: Well I don't mean to be disrespectful, but I think it takes a lot of talent to do the things Mark does. To me it was very impressive.

"The Swiss Aristocrat" Noah Peyrot: Impressive you say? Tell me something: were you impressed last week when I won my match with a simple, forearm to my opponent?

Super Stud: That is a good question, Eric!

Description of Visual: *As Mark is catching his breath, Sonny slowly pulls himself back to his feet.*
Before Sonny can react, Mark goes back on the attack. He strikes Sonny in the

jaw with a strong forearm.
Sonny fights to stay on his feet, and staggers away from Mark.

Eric: Mark is still not giving Sonny a chance to breathe.

Super Stud: No. But he better watch the referee's count.

"The Swiss Aristocrat" Noah Peyrot: I do not mean to be disrespect Mr. Stud, but I believe you forget that a count-out, would actually work in Mark's favor. Remember, a title can only change possession via either a pin-fall or a submission.

Super Stud: You're right, Mr. Peyrot! I did completely forgot about that! And please, just call me Stud.

"The Swiss Aristocrat" Noah Peyrot: I shall. And because of my respect for you sir, you may simply refer to me as Noah.

Super Stud: I shall.

Description of Visual: *Sonny turns around, hoping to fire off some form of attack.*
Mark drives the sole of his boot into Sonny's stomach, causing him to double over and clutch at his stomach.

Eric: And a kick to the gut by Mark!
Noah do you think…

"The Swiss Aristocrat" Noah Peyrot: Mr. Peyrot, if you please!

Eric: Sorry…*Mr.* Peyrot. Do you have a favorite to win.

"The Swiss Aristocrat" Noah Peyrot: I feel that since my… "transformation" and becoming aware of my true self, I now know what I have to do, to ascend to the top of the Alpha Wrestling Organization. Because of that, It is only a matter of time, before I compete for and obtain, the New Age Championship title.
So to answer your question, it matters, not who is the holder of that title.

Super Stud: Did you hear that? It matters, not!

Eric: I heard him, Stud.

Description of Visual: *Mark quickly traps Sonny in a front face lock.*
Sonny tries to get free but Mark grabs him by tights.
Mark lifts Sonny straight up in the air.

Eric: Suplex could be coming up.

Description of Visual: *Instead of falling backwards, Mark takes a few quick*
steps forward.
Mark then drops Sonny, stomach first, onto the ringside barricade.

Eric: Mark showing how strong he is with that one!

Super Stud: And how aggressive he is too!
That move will cause someone to lose their lunch.

"The Swiss Aristocrat" Noah Peyrot: Yes that was definitely a…vomit
inducing maneuver.

Description of Visual: *Sonny slides off the barricade, landing on his feet,*
before collapsing to the floor.
Sonny is now on the crowd side of the barricade. He is holding his stomach as
he lay in one of the big spaces without fans, that separates the sections of the
arena.

Super Stud: Sonny looks like a guy I knew after a weekend binder.

"The Swiss Aristocrat" Noah Peyrot: You know I've heard that you use to be
quite the card in the days of yester. .

Super Stud: I was quite the card! You might say I was a real…Joker.

"The Swiss Aristocrat" Noah Peyrot *[laughingly]***:** I say Stud, did you make a
funny? You sir are quite witty.

Super Stud: Thank you, Noah. Thank you.

Description of Visual: *While Sonny lay on the floor, Mark finally realizes that*
the referee has been counting he and Sonny out of the ring. He is unsure when
the referee had started counting, but he knows the referee's count is up to seven.
Mark slides back into the ring.

Mark then, slides right back out of the ring. Mark's quick entrance and quick exit, forces the referee to restart his count.

Super Stud: That didn't make sense.

"The Swiss Aristocrat" Noah Peyrot: I concur.

Eric: Why is that, Mr. Peyrot?

"The Swiss Aristocrat" Noah Peyrot: Because Stud is correct.

Eric: No, I mean why do you feel that that doesn't make sense?

"The Swiss Aristocrat" Noah Peyrot: Are you daft? We talked about this a little bit ago! Mark could have achieved a victory had he let the referee continue his count and retained his title! By him breaking up the count, he has given, Sonny an opportunity to recover and still has to continue competing!

Eric: You know, maybe Mark wants to defeat Sonny solidly, in the ring? Maybe he doesn't want to *just* win the match?

"The Swiss Aristocrat" Noah Peyrot: As far as I am concerned, a victory under any circumstances is still a victory.

Super Stud: That's right, Noah.
A win is a win, Eric.

"The Swiss Aristocrat" Noah Peyrot: Well said, Stud.

Description of Visual: *Sonny is still on the fan's side of the barricade and is beginning to pull himself back to his feet.*
Back on the ring side of the barricade, Mark has his hands on his knees and is waiting for the right moment to strike.

Eric: Mark seems to have something in mind.

"The Swiss Aristocrat" Noah Peyrot: Something unimpressive, I would imagine.

Description of Visual: *Mark feels that Sonny is now in the proper position, and is ready to strike.*

Mark begins to run towards Sonny.
When he is close enough, he leaps into the air and flies over the barricade.
He soars through the air.
He extends his arms.
He hits Sonny in the chest, just below the neck and knocks him to the floor.

Eric: Mark looked like an eagle the way he hit Sonny with that flying clothesline!

Description of Visual: *After hitting the clothesline, Mark manages to land on his feet.*
Unfortunately, Mark loses his footing. and stumbles past Sonny.
Mark tries to stay vertical, but ends up falling to the floor.

"The Swiss Aristocrat" Noah Peyrot: What a clumsy oaf.

Super Stud: I like that word. Oaf.

Description of Visual: *Despite being on the receiving end of Mark's attacks, Sonny still has some fight in him.*
Sonny manages to find the strength to roll onto his side.
He digs down deep inside of himself, and finds the strength to get onto his knees.
Mark is able to get back to his feet as well. As he starts making his way over to Sonny, we see that he is noticeably limping.

Eric: Mark may have twisted his ankle or something, when he landed after that clothesline.

Super Stud: It wouldn't have happened if he had let the referee count Sonny out.

"The Swiss Aristocrat" Noah Peyrot: Indeed. You are most correct.

Description of Visual: *Sonny watches as Mark limps over to him.*
When Mark reaches Sonny, he quickly grabs him by the side of the head.

Eric: That twisted ankle has really slowed things down.

"The Swiss Aristocrat" Noah Peyrot: Another reason all that flying is unwise.

Description of Visual: *Before Mark can execute his next attack, Sonny quickly*

scoops Mark off the floor.
Mark wiggles and tries to get free.
Sonny turns around and slams Mark onto the barricade.

Eric: Sonny with a powerful bodyslam!

Super Stud: Did you see the way Mark bounced off that barricade?

"The Swiss Aristocrat" Noah Peyrot: It was indeed impressive. It shows a level of savagery and even some levels of barbarism.

Description of Visual: *After bouncing off the barricade, Mark lands, stomach first on the ringside portion of the floor. There is great anguish displayed on Mark's face as he clutches at his lower back.*

"The Swiss Aristocrat" Noah Peyrot: If I'm not mistaken, it appears that Mark is on the verge of tears.

Super Stud: Well the way he landed, it wouldn't surprise me if he was about to cry. He could possibly have some spinal damage.

Description of Visual: *Mark tries to fight through the pain and get to his feet, but at the moment, he is unable to do so.*
The referee is unsure how serious Mark's injuries are and he quickly leaves the ring to check on him.

Super Stud: You know, we don't often talk about this, but if the the referee feels that Mark can't continue, Mark will not only lose the match, but the title as well.

Description of Visual: *On the other side of the barricade, Sonny is starting to get back to his feet. He's holding his stomach, with pain in his eyes as he tries to follow up on his attack.*

Eric: How hurt do you think Sonny is?

"The Swiss Aristocrat" Noah Peyrot: Well it appears as though he's having trouble erecting himself.

Eric: Excuse me?

"The Swiss Aristocrat" Noah Peyrot: I mean he's having trouble, standing up straight!
Please, refrain from being so vulgar!

Super Stud: Yeah Eric! Stop with the vulgarity!

Description of Visual: *As Sonny reaches the barricade, he sees Mark clutching at his lower back, pushing the referee away and trying to get to his feet. Sonny knows he has to stay on Mark and begin to pull himself up onto the barricade.*

Eric: Sonny getting ready to take a risk.

Description of Visual: *While Mark is getting back to his feet, Sonny is standing on the barricade, trying to balance himself.*
Mark begins to search for Sonny. He slowly turns around, still hurting and clutching at his back.
Before Mark can defend himself, Sonny front flips off the barricade and crashes, back first into Mark, knocking him to the floor.

Eric: Sonny throwing caution to the wind, knocking Mark down with a flipping senton!

Description of Visual: *The two competitors lay on the floor, trying to gather their wits.*

Super Stud: This match hasn't even gone that long and both of these guys already look like they've been in a war!

Eric: These two men…

"The Swiss Aristocrat" Noah Peyrot: Just a second, Eric.
Lord Manny, would you please go and check on those two?
Thank you.

Eric: And what is that about?

"The Swiss Aristocrat" Noah Peyrot: Oh, I merely want to know the condition of the competitors.

Eric: Really? Why?

"The Swiss Aristocrat" Noah Peyrot: Because I am concerned about their well-being.

Super Stud: Yeah, the man has a big heart, Eric! Why is that so wrong?

Description of Visual: *Both Sonny and Mark, slowly start to move.*
After thinking about it for a few seconds, the referee decides to restart his ten-count.
Before the count can begin, Lord Manny strolls into the scene and looks down on both Mark and Sonny.
As Lord Mark checks on Mark and Sonny's condition, the referee sees him, and yells "Get out of here! What are you doing anyway?"
Lord Manny does not put up a fuss. He raises his hands and slowly backs off.

"The Swiss Aristocrat" Noah Peyrot: Well that was rude on the referee's part.

Super Stud: It was. Lord Manny was doing nothing wrong at all.

Description of Visual: *Lord Manny returns to his spot, behind Noah.*
Noah slides his headset away from his ear.
Lord Manny whispers something into Noah's ear.

Eric: Any idea what their talking about?

Super Stud: No clue. And it's none of my business anyway!
Quit being so nosey!

Description of Visual: *Sonny and Mark begin to slowly get back to their feet.*
Sonny manages to get to his knees.
Mark, is on his hands and knees.

Eric: The desire that both of these men have, to be the New Age Champion is insane!
It really shows you how important that title really is!

"The Swiss Aristocrat" Noah Peyrot: I would actually agree with you on that, Eric.
But when *I* become the holder of that title, it will *really* mean something.

Super Stud: Wow! You said something that Noah agrees with. Good job, Eric.

Eric: Oh, thanks.

Description of Visual: *Sonny is able to get back to his feet.*
He is still clutching at his stomach, as he heads towards the ring.

Eric: Sonny about to beat Mark back into the ring.

Description of Visual: *While Sonny is rolling back into the ring, Mark is able*
to pull himself back to his feet.

"The Swiss Aristocrat" Noah Peyrot: If I were to venture a guess, I would say
that things are not going to go well for one, Mark Sandal.

Super Stud: Ya know, I'm inclined to agree with you, Noah.

Eric: Would you two care to discuss why you feel that way?

"The Swiss Aristocrat" Noah Peyrot: I would rather not.

Super Stud: Just wait. You'll see.
Description of Visual: *After managing to make it to the ring, Mark grabs the*
middle rope and strains as he climbs up onto the apron.
Mark is only able to get the top half of his body between the top and middle
rope, before Sonny quickly hits him with a dropkick to the face.

Eric: And Sonny getting the drop on Mark as he tries to reenter the ring.

Super Stud: That's what we were talking about! Mark left himself at a
disadvantage by entering the ring second.

"The Swiss Aristocrat" Noah Peyrot: Indeed.
And though it was not very gentlemen like, it was a smart attack.

Description of Visual: *Sonny's dropkick stuns Mark and he is unable to move.*
The bottom half of Mark's body is trapped on the apron and his upper body is
dangling on the middle rope, inside of the ring.

Eric: Mark now in a compromising position.

Description of Visual: *Sonny quickly takes advantage of Sonny's inability to move, and climbs onto the second rope, adjacent to Mark.*
After finding his balance, Sonny leaps off the ropes.
As Sonny lands, the back of his legs, collide with the back of Mark's head, driving Mark face first into the mat.

Eric: And a leg drop from the second rope onto Mark!

Super Stud: Sonny may have hurt himself on that move as well.

"The Swiss Aristocrat" Noah Peyrot: Landing on one's posterior from such an altitude, can be very problematic and painful.

Super Stud: You are absolutely right, Noah. A painful posterior can be a problem.

Description of Visual: *Despite the pain in Sonny's lower extremities, he manages to get back to his feet.*
Sonny gets close to Mark and grabs him around the waist.
Sonny knows he can't pin Mark while he's in the ropes and he drags him to the center of the ring.

Eric: Sonny getting Mark away from the ropes. Probably going for a pin.

"The Swiss Aristocrat" Noah Peyrot: With Mark compromised, it would behoove him to do so.

Super Stud: Behoove. I like that word. I may start using it more.

Eric: Really?

Super Stud: Yes. It behooves me to expand my vocabulary.
How was that, Noah?

"The Swiss Aristocrat" Noah Peyrot: Excellent effort, Stud.

Description of Visual: *After he reaches the middle of the ring with Mark, Sonny rolls Mark onto his back and goes for the cover.*
The referee checks Mark's shoulders.
He strikes the mat once.
He strikes it a second time.

Mark raises his shoulder off the mat before a third.

Eric: And Mark able to get his shoulder off the mat, just in time!

"The Swiss Aristocrat" Noah Peyrot: Sonny should have hooked the leg!

Super Stud: I was just about to say that!

"The Swiss Aristocrat" Noah Peyrot: Great minds think alike. Eh, Stud.

Super Stud: Indeed they do, Noah.

Description of Visual: *Sonny sits up on his knees. He is frozen with shock that Mark was not down for the count.*
Mark is feeling a lot of pain, in his face and lower back. Despite that pain, Mark tries to put some space between he and Sonny and starts crawling towards the corner to his right.

Super Stud: Sonny has Mark on the ropes! He needs to stay on him if he wants to win

Description of Visual: *Sonny manages to get past the shock and refocuses on Mark.*
Mark has now reached the corner.
Sonny sees Mark in the corner, still on his hands and knees and begins to make his way over to him.
Eric: Sonny taking your advice it seems.

Description of Visual: *When Sonny reaches Mark, he grabs him by the ankle.*

Eric: Sonny has Mark now!

"The Swiss Aristocrat" Noah Peyrot: Very good Eric. You came to that deduction all on your own.

Super Stud: One thing is for sure, Eric doesn't miss *anything*.

Eric: Thank you, St…

Super Stud: Although you did miss Sonny, not getting his shoulder up, the last time he and Mark faced each other.

Eric: Let's just focus on *this* amazing match, please!

Super Stud: Sure.
Just try not to miss anything this time.

Description of Visual: *While facing away from Sonny, Mark is able to get himself up, onto one foot.*
Mark begins to hop on his free foot to maintain his balance.

Eric: I'm not sure how Mark is going to get out of this one. But he may have something in mind.

"The Swiss Aristocrat" Noah Peyrot: Despite my disdain for his style. I will give Mark his due and say that he is a resourceful athlete.

Super Stud: Well that's really nice of you to say, Noah.

Description of Visual: *Mark continues hopping, building up some momentum.*
Mark leaps into the air.
Mark rotates his body, and drives his free foot into Sonny's chest.

Eric: What a counter by Mark!

"The Swiss Aristocrat" Noah Peyrot: Eh. Not bad.

Description of Visual: *Sonny stumbles backwards, before falling to the mat.*
Mark's body trembles as he struggles to pull himself to his feet.
While at his lower back, Mark looks over and sees Sonny getting back on his feet as well.

Super Stud: Sonny better watch out!

Description of Visual: *Sonny is still dazed but manages to staggers towards Mark.*

"The Swiss Aristocrat" Noah Peyrot: I wholeheartedly agree with you Stud. Sonny definitely needs to be on guard.

Description of Visual: *Mark shakes his leg, as though shaking the pain out of his ankle.*

Mark then tries to ignore the pain in his back, as he moves closer to the corner, that he is closest to.
Mark takes a deep breath and grabs the top rope.
Mark pulls himself onto the middle ropes.
In a single vault, Mark springs off the ropes.
The audience looks on in amazement, as Mark soars through the air.
Mark turns his body amd reaches back.
Just before landing, Mark strikes Sonny in the jaw with his forearm, and lands sideways on the mat.

Eric: And a springboard flying forearm by Mark, knocks Sonny onto his back!

Description of Visual: *Sonny lay motionless on the mat.*
The pain in Mark's back intensifies. Despite that pain, Mark is able to drag himself over to Sonny and go for the pin.

"The Swiss Aristocrat" Noah Peyrot and Super Stud: He should hook the leg!

Eric: Wow. You guys are speaking in stereo now?

Description of Visual: *After checking the shoulders, the referee strikes the mat once.*
Twice. But Sonny manages to pop his shoulder off the mat before the three.

Eric: And a two-count only! I actually thought Mark had him.

Description of Visual: *Mark is in disbelief that Sonny was able to kick out.*
He winces a little as he tries to and shutout the pain in his lower back and get back to his feet.
After getting to his feet, Mark starts to gingerly walk over to the corner,
Mark once again pulls himself up onto the second set of ropes.

"The Swiss Aristocrat" Noah Peyrot: This is a high reason why I question this man's intelligence. With his lower vertebrae problems, as well as the complications with his ankle, an areal maneuver would definitely be ill advised.

Super Stud: I agree.

Eric: The higher the risk, the higher the reward as they say.

"The Swiss Aristocrat" Noah Peyrot: Oh that is something only a dolt would say.

Super Stud: Yeah Eric! Only a dolt would say that!

Description of Visual: *Mark takes a second to find his balance.*
Sonny starts to get back to his feet but he is unsure about where Mark is.
Everyone begins to anticipate what impressive maneuver, Mark has in mind.

Eric: It looks like Mark's ready to fly.

Description of Visual: *Mark leaps off the ropes, legs spread apart as he soars*
towards Sonny.
Mark's intentions are to wrap his legs around Sonny's head, and flip him over,
onto his back. A move called a hurracanrana. But just as Mark's legs touch
Sonny's shoulders, Sonny grabs Mark by the waist and slams him to the mat.

Eric: And Sonny able to counter Mark, with power bomb!

"The Swiss Aristocrat" Noah Peyrot: Poor Mark. That slam is not going to do his back, any favors.

Eric: You sounded a little sarcastic, Mr. Peyrot.

"The Swiss Aristocrat" Noah Peyrot: Oh? Did I? I assure you, it was not at all intentional.

Eric: That smile on your face says otherwise.

Description of Visual: *After slamming Mark to the mat, Sonny collapses to one knee.*

Eric: Sonny has Mark down! But can he follow-up?

Description of Visual: *Sonny rubs his face and tries to regain his faculties.*
Sonny knows this is the opening he's been waiting for, and pulls himself back to his feet.

Eric: Is Sonny going to be able to capitalize?

Description of Visual: *Sonny grabs Mark by the ankles.*

Sonny lifts Mark's legs.
He takes a second.
Then, Sonny steps between Mark's legs with his left leg.

Eric: What's this Sonny's about to do?

Description of Visual: *Sonny wraps Mark's legs, at shin level, around his own leg.*
Then, Sonny steps over.
What Sonny has done, is cause Mark to flip over onto his stomach and into a prone position.
To add to Mark's discomfort, Sonny leans back and compresses Mark's lower back.

Eric: The move Sonny has Mark trapped in, has a couple of popular names. But if I'm not mistaken, the original name, is a Sasori-Gatame!

Super Stud: A what?

"The Swiss Aristocrat" Noah Peyrot: Stud, since my departure, I've studied multiple languages, with Japanese being one of them.. I believe what Eric said, roughly translates to "Scorpion hold."

Super Stud: Well whatever you call the move, I don't think Mark will last much longer in it.

Description of Visual: *The referee gets in front of Mark, so that he can hear if he's going to verbally submit.*
Sonny struggles to maintain the hold, as he pulls back on Mark's legs.
The pain in Mark's lower back is intense and he fights the urge to tap out.

Eric: Are we about to see Mark's reign as New Age Champion to come to an end?
Description of Visual: *Mark raises his hand, palm side down. He wants to slap the mat, but the thought of letting down his fans, as well as losing a chance to fight for the World title, are the two things preventing him from slapping the mat.*
As everyone anticipates what's about to happen, an outside party can be seen in the background.

Super Stud: Eric, who is that climbing over the barricade?

Eric: I'm not sure, but it looks like…

Description of Visual: *After getting a camera close to the person, we see that this person has long unkempt hair that is dyed red, with black tips. He has a dark black goatee and is wearing a pair of torn black jeans and a black leather jacket.*
This person stands six foot two-inches tall and has a robust figure.
It is the man known as, Payne.

Super Stud: I said it last week when he showed up and I'll say it now: Heeee's Heeere!

"The Swiss Aristocrat" Noah Peyrot: Indeed he is.

Description of Visual: *Payne stares at the action with his head tilted.*
A smirk draws itself on his face, before he slides into the ring.

Eric: No! Not like this!

Description of Visual: *Payne runs toward Sonny.*
Sonny is unaware of Payne's arrival and gets knocked to the mat by a punch to the side of the head.

Eric: Oh Come on! Are you serious?

Description of Visual: *The referee looks up and sees Payne stomp on Sonny's back.*
Based off of this, the referee has no choice but to signal for the bell and bring the match to a close.

Eric: I can't believe that this great competition is going to end this way!

Description of Visual: *Once he hears the bell, Payne turns his attention towards Mark.*
The referee anticipates Payne's attack and tries to stop him. A sinister glare from Payne, causes the referee to back off.

Super Stud: Payne's got that look in his eyes.

"The Swiss Aristocrat" Noah Peyrot: A look that means that he does not have the best of intentions in mind.

Description of Visual: *Payne looks down at Mark, who is clutching at his back and trying to get back to his feet.*
Payne is confident he has Mark where he wants him, and reaches down and grabs him by the hair.
With a tight grip on Mark, Payne snatches Mark off the mat.

Eric: Oh no!

Description of Visual: *Payne traps Mark in a front face lock.*
Fear takes over the arena as Payne grabs Mark by the tights.
Payne then, lifts Mark up, falls backwards and drives him head first into the mat.

Eric: And Payne hitting Mark with the "Goodnight Nobody!"

Super Stud: And nobody gets up from that!

"The Swiss Aristocrat" Noah Peyrot: Gentlemen, would you excuse me please?

Super Stud: Leaving so soon?

"The Swiss Aristocrat" Noah Peyrot: Yes. I believe I have…some business to attend to.

Description of Visual: *Payne slowly gets back to his feet with a look of sinister delight in his eyes.*

Eric: It sickens me how much Payne enjoys hurting people!

Description of Visual: *Payne slowly reaches his hand into his pocket.*
A pair of handcuffs are in Payne's hand as he pulls his hand out of his pocket.

Eric: Not this again!

Description of Visual: *Payne begins to place the links over his knuckles, but stops.*
Payne appears to have a feeling, that something isn't right.

Payne slowly turns around and sees that Sonny is back on his feet.

Eric: Payne may be in trouble here.

Description of Visual: *With his hand clutching the side of his face, Sonny stares angrily at Payne.*
Payne has a look of confusion on his face, as he stares back at Sonny.
Payne's expression slowly changes into a smile,
Sonny's expression to changes to confusion.

Super Stud: I think I know the business Noah had to attend to.

Description of Visual: *The audience tries to warn Sonny, but to no avail.*
Noah uses his cane to strike Sonny in the back..

Eric: What was that about?

Super Stud: I'm sure Noah had a good reason.

Description of Visual: *Sonny's body stiffens as he drops to the mat.*
as Payne looks at Noah with an emotionless stare, Lord Manny quicky enters the ring.
Noah looks back at Payne as he hands Lord Manny his cane.

Super Stud: This is interesting.

Description of Visual: *While Lord Manny wipes Noah's cane with a white handkerchief, Noah and Payne continue their stare off.*
After giving the cane what Lord Manny would consider a thorough wipe down, he hands the cane back to Noah.
Noah receives the cane.
Payne looks at Noah as Noah nods at him.
Before anything can transpire, Noah slowly exits the ring.

Eric: Could this be the start of some strange union between these two?

Super Stud: There have been stranger duos in the world of professional wrestling.

Description of Visual: *As Noah heads backstage, three officials head down the aisle.*

Eric: Well thankfully, this thing isn't going to get anymore out of hand.

Description of Visual: *The officials start ordering Noah to get backstage. Noah and Lord Manny offer up no resistance and calmly start to walk away.*

Super Stud: I don't know why the officials are being so mean to Noah and Lord Manny. They really are fine upstanding gentlemen.

Eric: Yeah sure they are.

Description of Visual: *As the officials start to enter the ring, Payne drops to the mat and slithers out of the ring.*

Eric: I just can't understand why Payne would disrupt this match!

Super Stud: like I said about Noah, I'm sure in his mind, it was a good reason.

Eric: I don't think there's anything good about that man.

Description of Visual: *After exiting the ring, Payne makes his way to the barricade.*
 As the fans vocalize their disdain for what he has done, Payne climbs over the barricade, to the wide open space, and starts heading away from the arena.

Eric: Well I hope Mark and Sonny are okay after that attack.

Super Stud: I'm sure they're fine. The "attack" wasn't that bad.

Description of Visual: *Worry for Sonny and Mark fill the arena.*
Seeing Sonny and Mark start to come around, begins to quell everyone's concerns.
Sonny is the first to move. He places his hand against his spine and struggles to get back to his feet.
Mark starts to move next, but he appears to be a little worse off. His eyes are a little glazed over and he appears to be disoriented.
While Sonny is back on his feet, Mark is on one knee, trying to recover.

Eric: Well that's good to see. I mean they're not at 100% but they are moving

Description of Visual: *The officials try to help Mark, but he politely motions for*

them to back away.

Eric: Mark wants to get to his feet on his own it would seem.

Description of Visual: *The primary official places his hand on Sonny's shoulder and ask if he's okay.*
Sonny aggressively pulls away.
There's a look of shock on the officials face, prompting Sonny to apologize.
Sonny clutches at both his stomach and abdomen, before the official he's fine.

Super Stud: Sonny appeared to be upset for a moment.

Eric: Probably just disappointment for the way things turned out.

Description of Visual: *Sonny can be heard on camera asking if they are going to restart the match.*

Eric: I would love to see these two continue to do battle, but I don't think Mark is in any condition to keep going.

Description of Visual: *The official looks down at Mark.*
Mark is still on one knee, and looking down at the mat, with his hand on his head.
Feeling that Mark is not in any shape to continue at this time, the official tells Sonny that he is not going to allow the match to restart.
Sonny is visibly furious by the news. He tries to hold it together but is not sure what to say or do.

Super Stud: Uh-oh. Is Sonny going to hit the official?

Description of Visual: *Sonny's expression changes. There is no longer anger, but disappointment on his face.*
Sonny lowers his head and slowly leaves the ring.

Eric: That's a real tough break for Sonny. Mark as well. I can only hope that we see these two go at it, one more time, without interruption.

Description of Visual: *While still on his knees and holding his head, Mark slowly looks up. He is just in time to watch as Sonny gingerly heads to the back. There is concern on Mark's face. There is also a feeling inside of Mark. A feeling that he has to do something about this situation.*

Eric: Well Stud, I'm being told that we're going backstage with Lawrence Michaels who is with, Jack Houston.
Lawrence are you there?

Scene Change:

Description of Visual: *Backstage, in front of the basement door. Lawrence Michaels is holding a microphone, and ready to speak with Jack Houston.*

Lawrence Michaels: I'm here Eric.
Jack, you requested this time, in this location. What's going on?

Jack Houston: What's going on is that I'm not going to put up with this and I'm about to rectify this situation!

Description of Visual: *Something catches Jack's attention.*

Jack Houston: As a matter of fact, I'm about to rectify it now!

Description of Visual: *Payne walks into the scene and has an exasperated look on his face.*

Payne: What are you doing here?

Jack Houston: I need to talk to you, and I know this is where you hang out!
Now, you answer *my* questions.
First of all, what are you even doing here? You're not scheduled to be here.

Description of Visual: *Payne smiles at Jack before responding.*

Payne: I just wanted to show up in case you needed a filler match. You never know when someone could get…hurt.

Description of Visual: *Jack has a stern look in his face.*

Jack Houston: You're trying to be funny? Okay!
Tell me something, what is your problem? The stunt you pulled in last week's triple-threat match! And now this week, interfering in that match! I need you to explain!

Description of Visual: *Payne sighs, while rolling his eyes.*

Payne: Why is everyone so upset about what I did last week? I didn't break any rules.
There were no rules to break!
I was in a match with two really powerful guys! I went to a level that they weren't prepared to go to! Which I told them I was going to!
And because of that, I won!
As far as me interfering in the match just now? Well there's an old saying Jack, "speak of the devil and he shall appear."

Jack Houston: I know the saying. But just what do you mean by that?

Payne: Mark called me out!
I thought about it. And then I decided to answer the call!
Maybe next time Mark wants to challenge me, he'll remember this moment and think twice about doing it.

Description of Visual: *Jack strokes his chin and nods.*

Jack Houston: Is that right?

Payne: Yeah it is.
And...uh, since you're here, *boss*, I want *my* shot at the title, against Mark, next week!

Description of Visual: *Jack places his hands on his hips, tilts his head and frowns.*

Jack Houston: Do you really think you're in a position to demand anything?
Listen, you know I do not tolerate people interfering in matches. Matches are to be settled between whatever parties are involved, and *only* those parties!

Description of Visual: *Payne sighs and rolls his eyes.*

Payne: Make your point, boss man.

Jack Houston: Make my point, huh?
Okay.
My point is this: because of your actions tonight, I've decided to use you as an

example. That is why you are indefinitely sus…

?????: Jack! Jack!

Description of Visual: *A man of average height with a slightly obese figure, runs into the scene. He has a buzz-cut hairstyle and is dressed in a blue sports jacket. He is also wearing a black button-up shirt, with the top three buttons open and a pair of blue jeans.*

Jack Houston: Chris I'm sorta in the middle of something. Can this wait?

Description of Visual: *The man who Jack has identified as Chris, catches his breath and then responds.*

Chris: I'm sorry for interrupting, but I know what you're about to do and it's not going to work.
I deal with people like this in my company all the time. Suspending him isn't going to work.

Description of Visual: *Jack folds his arms*

Jack Houston: Well what do you suggest I do?

Description of Visual: *Chris starts to smile.*

Chris: I suggest you make him wait.

Description of Visual: *Jack frowns with confusion.*

Chris: Listen, we were about to go talk to the fans. Lets go do that. After that, I'll tell you my idea.

Description of Visual: *Payne slowly slithers between Jack and Chris.*

Payne: Listen, boss and…whoever you are, you may want to tread lightly when dealing with me.

Description of Visual: *Jack and Chris practically ignore Payne and start to walk away.*
Payne places his hand on Chris' shoulder.
Chris looks at Payne's hand and slowly turns around.

Payne: I've noticed that you're not wearing a tie…sir. Good thing.

Description of Visual: *Payne leans in a little closer to Chris.*
He pats him on the chest and smiles ominously.

Payne: Someone may try to…*choke* you with it.

Description of Visual: *Jack swats away Payne's hand.*

Jack Houston: That's enough of that! I'll deal with you later!

Description of Visual: *Jack puts his hand on Chris' shoulder and quickly escorts him away.*
As Jack and Chris leave, Lawrence steps back in and ask one last question.

Lawrence Michaels: Payne, do you have any thoughts?

Description of Visual: *Payne slowly turns his head towards Lawrence.*

Payne: My thoughts?
Right now, my thoughts are…that you need…to move!

Description of Visual: *Payne stares angrily at Lawrence*
Lawrence is visually overtaken by fear. His hand starts to shake and he nervously backs away.
Not wanting to be left alone, the cameraman leaves as well, but catches a shot of Payne angrily entering the door to the basement.

Scene Change:

Description of Visual: *We return to the commentator's table, with Eric and Super Stud.*

Eric: Before we move on, I just wanted to let everyone know that Mark was able to get back to his feet and he made it backstage under his own power.

Super Stud: He was walking a little slowly and gingerly.

Eric: He was.

But he's going to be examined and hopefully we should have an update on his condition.

Super Stud: Yeah that's all well and good, Eric. But who was that Chris guy Jack was talking to backstage?

Eric: I guess we're about to find out.

Description of Visual: *We cut to the ring, with ring announcer Tony Anderson ready to make his next introduction.*

Tony Anderson: Ladies and gentlemen, would you please welcome to the ring, The Owner of the AWO, Jack Houston.

Description of Visual: *The sound of an up-tempo country instrumental begins playing throughout the arena.*
The fans rise to their feet and cheer as Jack and Chris, walk out onto the stage and head to the ring.

Super Stud: You think Jack owes that Chris guy money? I heard he has a gambling problem.
Jack I mean.

Eric: Cut it out, Stud.

Super Stud: I just hope he gets some help. Gambling addiction is a serious thing.

Eric: Jack doesn't have a gambling problem, Stud!

Super Stud: Enabling him isn't helping the problem, Eric.

Eric: You know he's going to hear this later, right?

Super Stud: Jack knows I like to joke.

Eric: Yeah well…

Super Stud: But having a gambling addiction is *not* a joke.

Super Stud: Maybe he's going to give away some money.

Eric: That would be nice.

Super Stud: Or he could be asking us for some money.
You know? Gambling and all.

Eric: Stop it with the gambling addiction!

Description of Visual: *Jack looks around, and takes in the admiration.*
He takes a deep breath and then addresses the audience.

Jack Houston: Thank you very much ladies and gentlemen.
In a few moments, two of the AWO's finest women wrestlers, will be competing in this ring.
But before they do, I need to take care of some business.
As you may recall, last week, I announced that in the coming weeks, we will be holding a 16 woman tournament, to crown the new, AWO Modern Marvel champion.
Well that tournament is going to take place, in five weeks.

Description of Visual: *The audience begins to applaud this announcement.*

Jack Houston: This is an invitational tournament, and will feature 12 of the AWO's best women's competitors.
But I also have 4 spots that I have elected to fill with women, from four different promotions.

Description of Visual: *Intrigue fills the arena. Jack continues.*

Jack Houston: Now don't get me wrong, I am very proud of the females on this roster. They are without question, some of the best on the planet. But I'm real big on giving people chances, and I want to give some people who aren't under my umbrella a chance at becoming the Modern Marvel Champion.

Description of Visual: *The fans once again, start to applaud.*

Jack Houston: Which brings me to why I'm out here.

Description of Visual: *A portion of the fans can be heard, cheering wildly. Jack smiles as he turns to face Chris.*

Jack Houston: Now for those that don't know, this man…

Description of Visual: *To Jack's surprise, a large portion of the fans start chanting, GSW…GSW…GSW…GSW.*
The smile on Jack's face gets bigger.

Jack Houston: It seems a lot of you do know this man.
But for those that don't, the man standing next to me is a really good friend of mine.
He is the commissioner of Garden State Wrestling.
Ladies and gentlemen, would you please give it up for, Chris O'Mealy.

Description of Visual: *The fans start to applaud.*
Commissioner O'Mealy looks around and raises his hand, acknowledging and appreciating their approval.

Super Stud: Commissioner O'Mealy? Sounds like a character in a comic book.

Eric: Come on, Stud. The man is our guest this evening.

Super Stud: He's Jack's guest! I didn't invite him! But those are some nice, expensive looking shoes he has on.

Description of Visual: *The applause dies down and Jack continues.*

Jack Houston: Now the reason Commissioner O'Mealy is here, is because one of the women on *his* roster, is going to compete in the Modern Marvel Invitational Tournament. In turn, one of the ladies on our roster, is going to compete, at an upcoming GSW special event called "Never Broken," which I encourage you all to check out. As a matter of fact, check out GSW as a whole.

Description of Visual: *Applause fills the arena once again.*

Super Stud: Can you believe that Jack is giving away this precious air time to this…Garden State Wrestling?

Eric: The world is big enough for more than the AWO, Stud.

Jack Houston: Now then, I want you all to meet the woman that will represent GSW. So Chris, if you wouldn't mind, would you do the honors and introduce her to the world.

Description of Visual: *Jack hands the microphone to Commissioner O'Mealy.*

Commissioner O'Mealy: Thanks Jack.
AWO fans how's it going?

Description of Visual: *The crowd gives a loud response.*

Commission O'Mealy: I can't hear you guys! How's it going?

Description of Visual: *The response is even louder this time.*

Commissioner O'Mealy: That's more like it!
Now I want you all to keep that same energy going, for one of the toughest and most popular GSW wrestlers.
Ladies and gentlemen, this is Shy-Digga!

Description of Visual: *A female's voice was heard all over the arena screaming,* DIGGA-DIGGA! *A hardcore, southern inspired hip-hop instrumental immediately kicks in.*
It doesn't take long for an African American lady, to walk out onto the stage. The lady is dressed in a lime green sparkly jacket, over a white t-shirt with the word DIGGA *all over the front. She also has on, tight black jeans and black high-top sneakers.*

Super Stud: Well look at her.

Eric: Oh no.

Description of Visual: *Shy starts to dance to the music.*
That same portion of fans chanting GSW earlier, are now chanting DIGGA DIGGAAAA in tune with the music.

Super Stud: And she dances too? She dances too! I don't know how much of this I can take.

Eric: Why don't you take it easy and calm down?

Description of Visual: *As Shy continues to dance her way to the ring, the crowd gets hype and dances to the music with her.*

Eric: One thing I will say is, she has a magnetic personality.

Super Stud: That ain't all she has.

Eric: You just can't turn it off, can you?

Super Stud: It's not that I can't, I just don't want to.

Description of Visual: *The music dies down as Shy-Digga enters the ring. Commissioner O'Mealy hands her the microphone so that Shy can, excitedly greet the crowd.*

Shy-Digga: AWO, what up y'all?

Description of Visual: *The crowd responds with excitement.*

Shy-Digga: That's what's up y'all! That's what's up!
Listen, I can't tell y'all how happy I am to be here. And yo, I can't wait to throw down with some of the ladies here in the AWO. Ya feel me?
But look, I know I ain't a AWO regular, but I want y'all to do me a favor, so I know you got my back. When I say, Digga-Digga, I need y'all to say it back! A'ight?
DIGGA-DIGGAAA!

Description of Visual: *A large portion of the crowd responds with a DIGGA-DIGGAAAA.*

Shy-Digga: DIGGA-DIGGAAAA

Description of Visual: *Even more fans respond with a DIGGA-DIGGAAAA.*

Shy-Digga: Yeah y'all! I love it. Thank you.

Description of Visual: *Shy hands the microphone back to Jack, who is grinning* *from ear to ear.*

Jack Houston: I love it when she does that.
Okay now listen, I'm going to allow Shy to stay at ringside and watch the next match. I want her to see up close the type of competition she's going to be dealing with in the tournament.

Description of Visual: *Jack turns towards Shy.*

Jack Houston: But Shy, I want you to behave okay? Please don't interfere in this match.

Description of Visual: *Shy smiles at Jack and draws a cross over her heart before responding.*

Shy-Digga: Jack, I love you baby. So I tell you what, if they don't start nothin', I won't finish nothin'. A'ight?

Description of Visual: *Jack smiles back at Shy.*

Jack Houston: That seems fair to me.
That's all I have for now, but you'll see me again later with another announcement.

Description of Visual: *As Jack prepares to leave, his uptempo country music begins to play.*
Jack stops and starts waving his hand under his neck.

Jack Houston: Stop the music please. Stop the music.

Description of Visual: *The music stops.*
The audience gets quiet.

Jack Houston: Excuse me, Jason in audio? Do me a favor please and play Shy-Digga's music please. I feel like dancing.

Description of Visual: *Shy's music kicks in and the fans get excited.*
Shy smiles and starts dancing which brings everyone to their feet.
As the music continues playing, Jack starts to dance with Shy.

Eric: Look at Jack, getting down!

Description of Visual: *Jack's movements look as though he is holding a huge spoon and rapidly stirring a huge bowl.*
Commissioner O'Mealy and all the fans, cheer and laugh at Jack, who is barely in rhythm but obviously having fun.

Super Stud: Jack better stop before he gives himself a heart attack.

Description of Visual: *Jack stops dancing, places his hand on his chest and starts to catch his breath.*
Shy starts to laugh and raises her hand.
Both Shy and Jack high-five one another.
After the impromptu "party," Jack, Shy and Chris start to leave the ring.

Eric: You never know what you're going to see at an AWO event.

Super Stud: That's for sure. From great wrestlers, to Aristocrats to dancing old men, we've got it all.

Eric: Yes.
Well as things settle down out here, let's send you backstage with Natasha Moore who is with, "The Sensational" Angel Young.

Scene Change

Description of Visual: *Backstage with the other AWO backstage correspondent, the blonde haired, five-foot four Natasha Moore.*
Standing next to Natasha is a thick Caucasian woman, with brown hair.
This woman is five-foot, six inches tall and is wearing a pair of pink and purple sunglasses, a dark purple jacket over a dark purple and white sports bra.
To complete the look, she has on a long pair of dark purple and white tights and a pair of black boots.

Natasha Moore: Thanks Eric.
Angel, you're about to take on one of the toughest women in the AWO, Lethal E. If you win this match, you will receive a special opportunity. What's going through your mind?

Description of Visual: *Angel has her hands on her hips and looks very disgusted by everything.*
She looks at Angel and tosses her hair.

She sighs before she responds.

Angel Young: Well if you must know, what's going through my mind is the fact that Jack is letting that…trash, Digga compete in an AWO tournament?

Scene Change:

Description of Visual: *Back in the arena, we see a shot of Shy-Digga who is heading to her seat at ringside.*
A close-up of Shy shows her looking both shocked and offended by what she just heard.
Before we cut back to Angel, we can read Shy's lips and see her say, "oh no she didn't!"

Super Stud: Uh-oh.

Scene Change:

Description of Visual: *Backstage, Angel looks as though she had a revelation.*

Angel Young: Wait a minute! Did you hear what I said?
Trash.
Digga.
Trash Digga!
Wow I am so witty!

Description of Visual: *Angel laughs at her own joke.*
Natasha does not seem amused.

Angel Young: Anyway, trash like her, doesn't deserve to be in the ring with someone like me.
And you know what? Neither does Lethal E.
She is just…a savage. She might even be below Trash Digga!
She's…scum
So, even though its on *short* notice, I'm going to make *short* work of Lethal E.

Description of Visual: *Angel laughs again.*

Angel Young: Wow, I'm really on a roll tonight. A sensational roll.

Description of Visual: *Angel laughs even harder as she walks off.*

Natasha looks annoyed at Angel.

Natasha Moore: I believe we're going over to Lawrence Michaels who is with Lethal E.
Take it away, Lawrence.

Scene Change

Description of Visual: *We are now in a different area backstage with Lawrence Michaels and a five foot tall, slim African American woman.*
The woman is wearing a black sleeveless robe, a black sports bra, outlined in brown, a matching pair of tights, black knee pads and black boots.
The woman's hair is long, black and braided and pony tailed. She is angrily bouncing on her toes and there is an intense frown on her face.

Lawrence Michaels: Thanks Natasha.
Lethal E, you just heard…

Description of Visual: *Lethal E swiftly raises her hand, stopping Lawrence from finishing his thought.*

Lethal E: I know what you're about to ask!
So, Ms. Angel don't think I deserve to be in the ring with her huh?
Ms. Angel thinks I'm scum huh?
Ms. Angel think she gonna make short work of me huh?
Well Ms. Angel do you know where I'm from?
Do you know what *I'm* capable of?
Ms. Angel I will end you MOTHA…

Description of Visual: *Lethal E stops and takes a deep breath.*

Lethal E: Let me chill.
I'll put it like this: girlfriend…you about to find out… that messin' wit me…can have LETHAL…consequences!

Description of Visual: *Lethal E storms off.*
Lawrence watches as Lethal E takes her leave.
As he turns his attention back to us, he appears to be slightly nervous.

Lawrence Michaels: Let's go back to the ring.

Scene Change

Description of Visual: *Back in the ring, with Ring Announcer Tony Anderson.*

Tony Anderson: Ladies and gentlemen, our next contest is a women's match, scheduled for one fall.
The winner of the match will receive a "special" opportunity.

Super Stud: I hope we finally find out what this special opportunity is. I'm tired of hearing about it!

Description of Visual: *A fast paced, pop instrumental starts playing throughout the arena.*
Everyone in attendance recognizes the music and begins to jeer the arrival of the first combatant.

Tony Anderson: Introducing first, combatant number one. She likes to say that she is from the sensational section of San Jose, and that she weighs a sensational, one hundred eighty five pounds. She is "The Sensational" Angel Young.

Description of Visual: *Angel struts out and arrogantly waves to the people. This is her way to show the people, that their negative reception, does not phase her.*

Eric: You know Stud, Angel may be making a mistake coming out here by her self.

Super Stud: I hate to agree with you, but I think you're right.

Description of Visual: *Angel strolls down the aisle toward the ring.*
A look of fear appears on her face.
She stops halfway down the ramp, when she sees Shy-Digga get out of her chair.

Super Stud: Shy-Digga better calm down. Otherwise, Jack may reconsider putting her in the Modern Marvel Invitational Tournament.

Eric: I think you're right, Stud.

Description of Visual: *As Shy-Digga storms towards Angel, we at home can hear her say, "who you callin' trash? You don't know me! I got yo trash!"*

Shy's attitude is on full display. Her neck is moving and her index finger is raised, as she closes in on Angel.

Eric: Shy-Digga is not willing to take any stuff from anyone!

Super Stud: No, but what she better take, is a seat.

Description of Visual: *The fans erupt at the thought of seeing Shy get her hands on Angel.*
Angel's expression changes and she starts to back away, as Shy gets closer.

Eric: Angel doesn't appear to want any part of Shy!

Description of Visual: *Commissioner O'Mealy quickly steps in and manages to keep Shy away from Angel.*
It is unclear what the Commissioner says to Shy, but he is able to get through to her.
Despite still being visibly fuming, Shy returns to her seat.

Eric: Angel better be glad that Commissioner O'Mealy is here.

Description of Visual: *Feeling confident that she is safe, Angel arrogantly waves at Shy.*
Angel then raises her fists and gestures as though she wants to fight.

Super Stud: Angel better stop. Do you see the look on Shy's face, I've seen that look on a woman's face before. It never ends well.

Description of Visual: *Shy is still visibly angry, but Commissioner O'Mealy is able to cool her down a little.*
Rather than "play" Angel's game, Shy remains seated, but she does say to Commissioner O'Mealy, "you betta get'er! You betta get'er!"

Super Stud: Here's a life lesson for you, Eric. If someone ever says, "you better get so-and-so" it would be in your best interest to *get* so-and-so to stop doing what they're doing.

Eric: This has been life lessons from Super Stud.

Description of Visual: *As Angel continues to antagonize Shy and Shy appears to be trying to ignore her, a strong hip hop instrumental starts to play.*

Eric: Uh-oh!

Description of Visual: *Everyone rises to their feet and cheers as the next competitor is announced.*

Tony Anderson: Competitor number two hails from Detroit, Michigan and weighs one hundred and thirty pounds. Here is, Lethal E!

Description of Visual: *Lethal E storms out onto the stage.*

Eric: Here she comes, Stud!

Super Stud: And she looks furious!

Description of Visual: *As Lethal E's music blares throughout the arena, Angel's expression has changed from playful and arrogant, to terrified.*

Eric: Angel appears to caught between a rock and a hard place.

Description of Visual: *Lethal E marches down the aisle, with her eyes locked on Angel.*
Angel runs to ring and slides under the bottom rope.

Super Stud: Listen, I'm a fan of Angel as much as the next guy but…

Eric: Angel doesn't have fans.

Super Stud: Anyway, what I was about to say was that I don't think it's a smart idea for her to hide in the ring when Lethal E, her opponent, is going to the ring!

Eric: I…I actually can't argue with that.

Description of Visual: *As Lethal E, closes in on the ring, Angel begins to beg her to calm down.*
Lethal E slides into the ring under the bottom rope.
Angel runs over to Lethal E and delivers a forearm shot to her back of her neck, before E can get to her feet.

Super Stud: I take it back, Eric! Angel's plan was brilliant!

Eric: It figures you would like what she did.

Description of Visual: *With both competitors in the ring, the referee calls for the bell and officially starts the match.*

<u>**AWO Women's Single's Match - The Winner Receives a Special Opportunity: "The Sensational" Angel Young vs. Lethal E**</u>

Eric: Well despite how unfair Angel's attack was, this contest is underway.

Super Stud: Eric, don't start whining about fair and unfair! Lethal E wanted to get her hands on Angel! Lethal E was ready to compete! And Lethal E got into the ring under her own power! Lethal E took her eyes off the target and it costed her! Lethal E has no one to blame but herself!

Eric: Okay! Okay! I get it! But I still don't like it!

Description of Visual: *Lethal E is still on her knees.*
Angel continues to pound on E's back, preventing her from getting to her feet.

Eric: And Angel really laying into E!

Description of Visual: *Angel gets to her feet quickly, removing her jacket at the same time.*
Angel throws the jacket down onto E.
Lethal E is unable to defend herself, as Angel returns to raining down on her with forearm shots.

Super Stud: Ya know, despite no one knowing what this special opportunity is, Jack doesn't hand these out all the time, so it's gotta be a big deal.

Eric: That's true, Stud.

Description of Visual: *Lethal is still on her hands and knees.*
Angel gets back to her feet once again.
As Angel begins to stomps on E's back, she yells at Lethal E, "you don't deserve to be in here with me!"

Eric: I really don't think taunting E is a good idea.
Description of Visual: *Angel stomps on E's back once again. This time she*

yells, "Did you hear me? You don't deserve to be in here with me!"

Super Stud: I'm going to be honest, I sometimes forget how aggressive Angel can be.

Eric: She's as aggressive as she is, arrogant.

Description of Visual: *Angel points to Shy-Digga and yells, "you're trash just like her!".*
We cut to a shot of Shy, who looks irritated by Angel.

Eric: I can't understand why you would want to get two woman mad at you.

Super Stud: I've done it before and I'd rather not say what happened.

Description of Visual: *As Angel marches to the center of the ring, something snaps inside of Lethal E. She sits up on her knees and aggressively flings off Angel's jacket.*

Eric: Uh-oh. This may not go well for Angel.

Description of Visual: *Seeing the anger in Lethal E's eyes, gives Angel some concern. She decides that she has to get back on the offense and charges at E.*

Eric: Angel once again on the attack!

Description of Visual: *Angel leaps into the air, raises her right foot and tries to drive her boot into E's chest.*
In an impressive show of speed and strength, Lethal E catches Angel's foot.
E grabs Angel by the ankle, and prevents her from getting free.

Eric: I think E has had enough, Stud.

Super Stud: I'd say Angel should run, but…I don't think she can.

Description of Visual: *While still holding onto Angel's ankle, Lethal E slowly gets to her feet. As she prepares to retaliate, there's a look on E's face that tells us, she's going to enjoy what she's about to do.*

Super Stud: What do you think she's going to do?

Eric: Whatever it is, it can't be good.

Description of Visual: *E throws down Angel's foot.*
Angel loses her balance.
Lethal E extends her arm, runs at Angel and hits her in the chest.

Eric: And Angel taken off her feet by a lethal clothesline from Lethal E!

Super Stud: Lethal lariat is what you should've said.

Eric: From what I understand, a clothesline knocks you down, while a lariat knocks you out!

Super Stud: Alright, I'll give you that one.

Description of Visual: *Angel is able to get back to her feet but she is confused and dizzy.*
Lethal E takes advantage of Angel's disorientation, and once again clotheslines Angel to the mat.

Eric: And Lethal E has Angel in trouble now!

Description of Visual: *It took a little longer but Angel is able to get back to her feet. and she feels even more dizzy than before.*
Lethal E decides to use a different attack. She scoops Angel up and slams her to the mat.

Super Stud: The second bodyslam we've seen this evening! It's an old school move and it's effective! Very effective!

Description of Visual: *As the fans start to cheer for Lethal E, she looks around and takes it in .*

Eric: The fans are solidly behind Lethal E!

Super Stud: Are they behind her or scared to boo her?

Description of Visual: *As Lethal E refocuses on the match, Angel slowly sits up off the mat.*
Angel's pain can be seen all over her face. And she knows that she needs time to

recover.
As Angel starts to crawl towards the ropes, Lethal E rubs her hands together
and follows behind her opponent.

Eric: Lethal E, now in pursuit of Angel.

Super Stud: I can't tell you how scary that woman is. Reminds me of an ex-girlfriend I had, when she caught me with another ex-girlfriend I had.

Eric: I…wow. Just wow.

Description of Visual: *After Angel reaches the ropes, she pulls herself up to her feet.*
Angel slowly turns around and tries to gather herself.
When Angel turns around, she sees that Lethal E has her eyes locked on her and she knows that she is in trouble.

Super Stud: You ever seen the face of a lion, when it finds it's prey?

Eric: I have!

Description of Visual: *Angel raises her hands and begins to beg E to stop.*

Eric: I don't think begging is going to work with this lioness.

Super Stud: Probably not.
And don't call Lethal E a lioness. There's only one sexy lioness in the AWO.

Eric: Oh I beg your pardon.

Description of Visual: *Lethal E looks taken aback by Angel's begging. She says to Angel, "Oh you scared now," as she continues to move in.*
Angel continues begging.
Just as Lethal E reaches her, Angel throws a kick at her stomach.

Super Stud: Okay I'm sorry but didn't she learn the last time she tried to kick E?

Description of Visual: *Lethal E once again catches Angel's foot.*
Before Lethal E is able to attack, Angel grabs the ropes.
The referee steps in and warns E to put down Angel's foot.

Super Stud: Good call by the referee!
Just a reminder, Angel is in the ropes and the match can't continue until both competitors are in the center of the ring.

Eric: Yes, that is correct, Stud.

Description of Visual: *As the referee continues to warn Lethal E, Angel takes her thumb and pokes E in the eye.*

Eric: Are you serious? What an underhanded tactic!

Super Stud: It was self defense, Eric! Lethal E wasn't listening to the ref, so Angel had to do something!

Description of Visual: *Lethal E grabs at her eyes, and involuntarily turns away from Angel.*
The referee warns Angel about her action, but Angel ignores him.
Angel quickly moves close to Lethal E.
Angel leaps into air.
Angel grabs Lethal E's head and pulls her backwards.
As Angel lands on her side, she drives the back of Lethal E's head into the mat.

Eric: Angel calls that the "Halo breaker!"

Super Stud: Yes she does and she hit it in impressive fashion!

Description of Visual: *The audience is upset by what just happened and they try to rally their support for Lethal E.*
As quickly as she can, Angel goes for the pin.
The referee gets into position.
He slaps the mat once.
Twice.
A third time.
The referee gets up and signals for the timekeeper to ring the bell.

Eric: That's it! Lets get the official word!

Tony Anderson: Here is your winner, "The Sensational" Angel Young!

Eric: I have to admit, I'm surprised by this outcome.

Super Stud: I'm not. Angel is a top contender to the title, and a very crafty wrestler.

Eric: If by "crafty" you mean dirty, then I guess you're right.

Super Stud: Dirty? That woman is cleaner than fresh laundry! She smells like sunshine, she's so clean!

Eric: I'm not sure what to say to that. So let's move on.

Description of Visual: *As Angel gets back to her feet, the referee grabs her by the wrist and attempts to raise her arm, to signifying she's the winner.*
Angel is repulsed by this and snatches her arm away from the official.

Super Stud: Come on referee! You don't put your hands on Angel, unless she ask you to.

Description of Visual: *Angel looks down at Lethal E and squats down next to her.*
She grabs E by the cheeks and smiles as she begins to taunt her.

Eric: Can you explain this, Stud?

Super Stud: Sometimes you gotta rub it in to prove your point.

Eric: I just knew you would have an answer!

Description of Visual: *As Angel continues to taunt Lethal E, Shy-Digga slides into the ring.*

Super Stud: Hey wait a minute! She has no business getting in an AWO ring! I mean she…she doesn't work here, Eric!

Eric: Well whether she competes here or not, it looks like she's had enough.

Description of Visual: *After quickly getting to her feet, Shy pushes Angel off of Lethal E.*
Shy expects Angel to try something and waits for her to retaliate.

Eric: What's Angel going to do now?

Description of Visual: *Angel looks up at Shy with an expression made up of embarrassment and anger.*
Shy is still ready in case Angel wants to fight.
Angel looks around and sees all of the fans cheering with anticipation of this inter-promotional battle.

Eric: The fans want it? Are they going to get it?

Description of Visual: *Angel gets to her feet, with her fist raised, for a fight.*
Shy does not back down, and beckons for her to bring on the fight.

Super Stud: I think we are going to get it, Eric!

Description of Visual: *With her fist still raised, Angel continues to look at Shy.*
She cocks back her fist and gets ready to throw a punch.
To everyone's surprise, Angel rolls her eyes, and brushes Shy off.
Then, she turns away from Shy and walks away.

Eric: Well I guess we're not going to get it after all.

Super Stud: There's no need for Angel to fight Shy tonight anyway. Angel has already had and won her match.

Description of Visual: *As Angel heads to the ropes, Shy looks out at the fans and sees them vocalizing their disappointment.*
Believing that Shy is distracted, Angel runs at Shy and tries to throw a punch at her jaw.

Eric: Wait a minute! What's this?

Description of Visual: *Shy is able to anticipate Angel's attack and quickly ducks the punch.*
Shy quickly wraps her arms around Angel, from behind.
Then Shy lifts Angel up and throws her back first to the mat.

Eric: What a take down by Shy!

Description of Visual: *Angel tries to escape Shy's fury.*
Shy quickly mounts Angel, and immediately starts raining down rapid punches.

Eric: Shy is making Angel regret coming at her!

Description of Visual: *The fans cheer wildly at the beating Shy is giving Angel. Not wanting Shy to get into trouble, Commissioner O'Mealy slides into the ring and lifts her off of Angel.*
Shy is kicking and screaming, doing whatever she can to get free of Commissioner O'Mealy's grip. The commissioner refuses to let her go, which allows Angel to escape.

Super Stud: Run Angel! She's crazy! Run!

Description of Visual: *After Angel reaches the floor, she scurries to the ramp. The fans continue to cheer and even mock Angel as she makes her retreat. Meanwhile, Commissioner O'Mealy sets Shy down. He's still holding onto her waist, and trying to calm her down.*
Shy is still in fight mode but remains in the ring.
She screams at Angel, "come on back, girl! Come on back!" *as she beckons for her to return.*
Angel wants no part of this and continues back pedal to the backstage area.

Super Stud: That Shy is a firecracker, isn't she?

Eric: I guess you could call her that. I can't wait to see what she's going to do in the Modern Marvel Invitational Tournament.
At any rate, I want to remind you all, that in just a little bit, we will see the Titans of Tomorrow, taking on the Sixth Street Soldiers in a tag team contest. And while I'm on the subject of tag teams, I'm being told that there is a new team on it's way to the AWO and they've sent in a video that we're going to share with you all, right now.

Super Stud: I was in a video once.

Eric: Really?

Super Stud: Yeah with that ex-girlfriend I told you about earlier.

Eric: *[Sighs]* Let's go to the footage.

Scene Change

Description of Visual: *The screen goes black.*
The words, **FRO BROs** *flash across the screen.*
The words dissolve off the screen.
A multicoloured, psychedelic background, fades in on the screen.
As we pull back, we see the smiling faces of two Caucasian gentlemen. The men are are wearing sunglasses and sporting afro hairstyles.
As we continue to pull back, we see that the men are wearing white t-shirts with an afro logo on the chest and black pants tucked into black boots.
The man on the right looks to be about 6'4 and a muscular 230lbs. His name, **Lt. Fro,** *appears on the screen.*
Standing next to him is a man who appears to be a couple inches shorter, but also has a muscular build. Right beneath him, his name, **Sgt. Fro,** *appears on the screen.*
The two men stare at us, before Lt. Fro *excitedly speaks.*

Lt. Fro: Aloha!

Description of Visual: *The word* **ALOAH** *fades onto the screen.*
The word fade.
Lt. Fro continues to speak.

Lt. Fro: We're the Fro Bros! And we would like to welcome you, to the light side!

Description of Visual: *Lt. Fro waves his hand majestically in front of him. A bold, neon yellow logo that says* **LIGHT SIDE** *appears on the screen.*
The logo disappears as Sgt. Fro pulls Lt. Fro's hand down.

Sgt. Fro: Enough with the pleasantries Lieutenant, let's get to the point!

Description of Visual: *A finger pointing at the camera, blinks on the screen.*

Lt. Fro: You're right Sarge, my brother. Let's get down to business!

Description of Visual: *Lt. Fro's face changes to a more serious expression.*

Lt. Fro: We've noticed that the AWO tag team division could use a…shot in the arm!

Description of Visual: *A black and white photo of someone getting an injection in the arm appears behind the two men.*

Sgt. Fro: Seriously! I mean look at the current tag champs for instance! Not only are they an insult to the AWO fans, but they're a couple of as…

Lt. Fro: Sarge, you can't say that! There's kids out there man!

Sgt. Fro: I can't say asphole?

Lt. Fro: That's not a word.

Sgt. Fro: Sure it is.

Description of Visual: *Blinking on the screen is a disclaimer.* **ASPHOLE IS NOT AN ACTUAL WORD.**

Lt. Fro: Anyway!

Sgt. Fro: Yes, anyway.
When we get to the AWO, what you thought you knew about tag team wrestling, is going to change…

Lt Fro: Change Froever now.

Sgt. Fro: And change Froever more.

Both: Maholo!

Description of Visual: MAHOLO *appears on the screen.*

Fade to black

Scene Change

Description of Visual: *We fade in on the commentator's table, with both Eric and Super Stud looking into the camera.*
Eric appears to be delighted with what he just saw.
Super Stud seems confused.

Super Stud: I…uh…I'm not sure what to make of that. I mean where did the…Fro Bros even come from?

Eric: Spadamack Championship Wrestling.

Super Stud: Spada what?

Eric: Spadamack Championship Wrestling. The owners of the company combined their names, Spencer, Adam and Zack and formed, Spadamack. It's no longer in business, but they had a cult following, a few years ago.

Super Stud: I see.
I got a strange feeling about the…Fro Bros.

Eric: Well they did do some strange things in Spadamack Championship Wrestling.
Anyway, I'm being told that we are going backstage once again, with Jack Houston.

Scene Change

Description of Visual: *Backstage, inside of Jack Houston's office.*
Jack is standing in front of his desk, ready to once again address the audience.

Jack Houston: Hello again, everyone!
Remember when Eric told you all earlier, that we were going to need your help with something? Well, it's time for me to explain.
Now, you all heard me talking about the Modern Marvel Invitational Tournament coming up. Twelve women wrestlers from the AWO and four women selected from four different promotions. Well you met Shy-Digga from Garden State Wrestling, and you got just a taste of how bad she can be. Next week, you're going to meet the representative from a company known as the Championship Wrestling Federation.
But right now, I want to talk about the AWO portion of the tournament.
I'm going to be completely transparent with you all, I've got eleven of the twelve, AWO women decided for the tournament. But I'm having a tough time deciding who number twelve will be. I have it narrowed down to four women, and while I could have easily made a four-way match between the four ladies, I want you guys' input.
Here's how.
Those of you in the arena, if you look in front of your seat, you'll see a device. That device will allow you to vote for the person, you would like to have the final spot in the Modern Marvel Tournament.
Those of you at home, I want you guys to participate as well. Just call the

number on your screen and when prompted, select the woman that you want to get the last spot in the…

Angel Young: Jack! Jack!

Description of Visual: *Jack's attention is now on Angel as she barges into the scene.*

Jack Houston: Um…Angel, I'm in the middle of something. Can't this wait?

Description of Visual: *Angel rolls her eyes at Jack.*

Angel Young: No Jack, this can't wait!
I want to know why you allowed that Trash Digga girl here in our company? I mean she's so beneath our standards.

Description of Visual: *Jack takes a deep breath and tries to keep his composure.*

Jack Houston: Well I don't care for, or agree with the words you're using. But you do ask a good question. And in a way, I'm sure it's on the mind of a lot of people.
Well, the reason I opened this tournament up to women that are not signed to the AWO, is because the four companies they work for, are owned by four of my closest friends. Because of that, I want to give their companies some publicity. It's that simple.
To me, the AWO may be the Alpha of wrestling. But there are other "worlds" of wrestling. Those worlds have some pretty talented women wrestlers. And I wish all the women in the tournament, the best of luck. Including you, Angel.
And by the way, I plan on doing other inter-promotional events.

Description of Visual: *Angel rolls her eyes and flicks her hair.*

Angel Young: *[Sarcastically]* Wow Jack, that was some speech. And just so you know, nobody calls me "Sensational" because I'm…lucky.

Description of Visual: *Jack lets out a deep exhales before responding.*

Jack Houston: I see.
Well, we'll find out how *Sensational* you are, when you compete in the tournament.

Description of Visual: *Angel smiles arrogantly.*

Angel Young: Yes we will.

Description of Visual: *Jack smiles back at Angel.*

Jack Houston: And at the same time we'll find out if Shy-Digga really is "beneath you."

Description of Visual: *Angel's smile slowly fades off of her face.*

Angel Young: What do you mean?

Jack Houston: Well I was going to bring this up in just a moment. But I'll do it now.
I don't know if you were paying attention, but it was said multiple times, that the winner of you and Lethal E's match would receive a special opportunity. Well that special opportunity is that, in the first match of the Modern Marvel Invitational Tournament, you, Angel Young, are going to take on…Shy-Digga.

Description of Visual: *Angel becomes visibly angry.*

Angel Young: What?

Jack Houston: Yeah!
And since you're so confident that Shy is "beneath you," you shouldn't have any trouble beating her.

Description of Visual: *Angel's body starts to tremble.*

Angel Young: But…but…but…

Description of Visual: *Jack leans in close to Angel.*

Jack Houston: Is there a problem?

Description of Visual: *Angel let's out a grunt of frustration as she storms out of Jack's office.*
Jack watches Angel's departure and smiles playfully at her rage.

As Jack tries not to laugh, he returns his attention back to us, the viewers.

Jack Houston: She sure is something.
Anyway, back to the voting talk.
I encouraged the four women up for consideration, to make videos pleading their case. To my surprise, none of them disappointed. One of them even features a cameo that I was not prepared for.
At the conclusion of the fourth woman's comments, voting will begin. You will have until the conclusion of the final match, to vote. I'll be back at the end of the night with the results, and some more announcements.
But right now, take a look at these.

Scene Change

Description of Visual: *We are now looking at a full-figured, Caucasian woman. The woman has short brown spiked hair and is wearing a sleeveless black t-shirt. Her arms are exposed and we can see that she has a sleeve of tattoos on her right arm. She is also wearing a pair of black basketball shorts.*
The woman is pacing back and forth. And with every passing second, she appears to be growing more and more agitated.
Suddenly, she stops.
She turns towards the camera. And as she begins to speak, her name appears on the screen.

Kelly Bowens: So let me get this straight: Jack Houston wants me to…*plead* my case and leave *my* future in the hands…of *you* people?

Description of Visual: *Kelly's frown intensifies as her frustration appears to grow.*

Kelly Bowens: KellyBowens, doesn't plead for nothin'!
I want you dum-dums to listen up!
If you know what's good for you, you'll vote me into that tournament!
If you don't, I swear on everything, something bad will happen to someone you love!

Description of Visual: *We fade out on a shot of Kelly looking angrily into the camera.*

Scene Change

We fade in on a shot inside of an old gym.

There's an old wrestling ring inside of the gym.
A dark haired, Caucasian woman, is siting on the apron portion of the ring, with her head down.
The woman is wearing a black sleeveless hooded sweatshirt, a pair of black athletic shorts and a pair of black sneakers.
As she raises her head, her name appears on the screen.

"The Unbreakable" Brenda Steel: Sometimes I come to this gym, not just to train, but to think.
When I got here today, I started to thinking about…about how I got here. By here I mean, having to get *voted* into a tournament.
I should be a shoe-in.
I should be a champion.
But I'm not.
And why?
Why am I not a champion?
Why am I not even a top contender to the title?
Why wasn't I *given* a spot in the Modern Marvel Invitational Tournament?
The answer is...because I don't deserve it.
Now I don't know what's been holding me back.
But you know what?
It stops now!
And whether or not I get voted in, from this day forward, I am going to show the world…that I will not, be broken.

Description of Visual: *We fade out on a shot of Brenda looking very serious into the camera.*

Scene Change

Description of Visual: *We fade in on a shot in front of a tall, chain link fence. In front of the fence is a rugged looking woman, standing sideways with her hand on the fence.*
Her hair is short, bleached blonde and slick back.
She appears to be about 5'6 tall and her athletic shape, is covered by a tank top, that looks like the flag of Ireland.
She is also wearing a pair of black jeans, and a pair of loosely tied black boots.
As she looks at us, her name appears on the screen. And with a prominent Irish accent, she speaks.

Fiona McCarthy: I'm suppose to try and convince you dopes to vote for me! You know what? I'm gonna tell you, *not* to vote for me!

Description of Visual: *Fiona turns and faces the camera.*

Fiona McCarthy: Not because I don't deserve to be in the tournament. Because having to get *voted* in has made me so mad, whoever I'm in the ring with, is going to get hurt!
So do the other lasses a favor, and don't make me hurt them. Because I would hate for someone's career to be over, because of all of you.

Description of Visual: *Fiona is breathing heavily as she stares intensely into the camera.*

Scene Change

Description of Visual: *We transition to a shot of a slim, Caucasian female with brownish red hair, sitting on the porch of a rustic log cabin.*
She is wearing a red sweat suit and appears to be reflecting on something.
As she looks at us, and prepares to speak, her name appears on the screen.

Trisha "Chernobyl" Noble: This is my grandparents' cabin. I come up here sometimes to get away from everything. When I don't want to be "Chernobyl" and just be Trisha.
I've been up here ever since I lost to Tamara. I guess I came up here…cause I was mad at myself.
I wasn't mad because I lost. That's going to happen. I was mad because, I didn't know why I lost.
I didn't know why I lost my head.
I didn't know why I lost myself.
Since I've been up here, I've had time to think.
Time to reflect.
  Time to look within.
I figured it out.
I know what happened now.
I got scared.
Scared I was going to let everyone down.
Scared I wouldn't be able to live up to expectation.
Scared of failing in front of the world.
But then, I talked to a friend.
A good friend.
A good friend that helped me get through this.
A good friend that helped me get my spark back.
Listen, I'm suppose to be asking you guys to vote for me or something

but…honestly, it doesn't feel right for me to do that.
I had my shot at the title and I blew it. But…

????: She may not feel right about it, but I do!

Description of Visual: *We soon see Lola walk out of the cabin.*
As Lola moves behind Trisha, we see that she is dressed in a purple hooded sweat shirt over a white t-shirt. She also has on a pair of black baggy cargo pants and a pair of black boots.
Lola is also wearing a pair of sunglasses.
As she removes the glasses, we see that the area around her left eye, is seriously bruised and greatly swollen.
Trisha looks up at Lola and starts to speak.

Trisha: Lola you don't have to…

Description of Visual: *Lola cuts Trisha off by placing a hand on Trisha's shoulder and sighs.*
Then, Lola starts to speak.

Lola: Listen, this girl right here is my best friend. She is the sweetest and humblest person I know. She's not going to ask you to vote for her.
But I am.
She deserves to be in the Modern Marvel Invitational Tournament.
She deserves to be the Modern Marvel champion.
So please, as a favor to me, vote for Trisha. So that the first ever Modern Marvel champion, can be someone *we* can be proud of.
And don't worry about me, everyone. I will heal. I will be back. And I promise you Dale, you will definitely get what's coming to you.

Scene Change

Description of Visual: *The screen fades to black.*

YOU MAY BEGIN VOTING NOW

appears on the screen.
We transition back to the arena, where we see fans beginning to vote.
We fade in on Eric and Super Stud, who are at the commentator's table ready to speak.

Eric: So Stud, who would you like to see get voted into the Modern Marvel Invitational Tournament?

Super Stud: Fiona McCarthy! Or Kelly Bowens!

Eric: Really?

Super Stud: Yeah! I like their styles! They're both no nonsense competitors. And they're good at hurting people.

Eric: I see.

Super Stud: Are we allowed to vote?

Eric: No.
But what we can do, is show everyone some comments, made by the Sixth Street Soldiers.
Then, we'll show everyone some comments from the Titans of Tomorrow. Both of which, were recorded earlier today.

Scene Change

Description of Visual: *We are staring at three individuals; two men and a woman.*
Sitting in a metal folding chair, is a Caucasian male with an athletic figure and a rectangular body type. Had he been standing, we'd be able to tell that he is about six feet, two inches tall.
He is wearing a black vest, outlined in brown, which covers up the tattoos all over chest and stomach. He is also wearing a pair of brown camouflage pants tucked into a pair of black boots. To complete the look, he is wearing a brown shemagh, which covers his entire head, except for his eyes.
He is rubbing his hands intensely and his body is slightly swaying side to side.
Stand to the man's right is the other Caucasian male. He has a strongman physique with an oval shaped body type. He has a long, thick brown, beard and appears to be about six feet three inches tall.
His outfit, matches his partners except replacing the shemagh is a black boonie hat.
He looks to be very intense and is growling as he flexes his muscle.
The woman of the group is standing behind the man in the chair, to the left. She is slightly shorter than her male friends but is in tremendous shape.
She has dark black hair, with the tips dyed pink, and is wearing a black vest outlined in brown over a black sports bra and black tights. She is also wearing

IT'S
TIME

As the gentleman in the chair removes the wrap from his mouth and prepares to speak, his name appears on the screen.

Hagan Benally: People like to ask us, why we call ourselves the Sixth Street Soldiers.
Well where we grew up, Sixth Street, it was like boot camp for life.
Sixth Street was in the part of town that the…"*less fortunate*" people lived.
When the "better-offs" heard you were from Sixth Street, they looked down on you.
They mocked you.
They made you feel like you were less than people.
Well one day, we decided to fight back and show those clowns that they weren't better than us.
That their money didn't make them better.
Today, we don't want to just show the better-offs. We want to show everyone that if you look down on us…we will PUT…YOU…DOWN!
People wonder why we call ourselves "soldiers."
Soldiers are known for fighting. And anyone that grew up on Sixth Street knows, you gotta fight for everything. And if it's one thing we've come to enjoy…it's fighting!
Speak to'em Evan!

Description of Visual: *The big man behind Hagan stops flexing.*
He looks towards us and laughs maniacally.
After he stops laughing, his name appears on the screen, and in a loud voice, he speaks.

Evan Skaggs: TONIGHT, WE GET ONE STEP CLOSER TO BECOMING THE AWO WORLD TAG TEAM CHAMPSIONS!
TONIGHT, WE SHOW THE TITANS OF TOMMORW, THAT YOU DON'T MESS WITH ANYONE FROM SIXTH STREET!
AND AFTER GOING TO WAR WITH THE TITANS, EVERYONE WILL FIND OUT THAT THERE'S TOUGH…AND THEN THERE'S SIXTH STREET TOUGH! RIGHT CALI?

Description of Visual: *As Evan laughs manically, the woman of the group looks at us intensely with her arms folded.*
As her name appears on the screen, she begins to address us.

Cali Ivey: That's right Evan!
And not only are you *two* going to show everyone, but soon, I'm going to show everyone as well.
I'm putting the Women's Division on notice, Cali Ivey…is coming!

Description of Visual: *Hagan rises out of his chair*
He slides it out of frame and looks at us intensely.

Hagan Benally: Sixth Street, no more talk!
Sixth Street, no more games!
Sixth Street Soldiers… IT'S…TIME!

Scene Change

Description of Visual: *We transition to a locker room setting, where we see two big Samoan gentlemen, sitting next to each other on a bench.*
Both men have strongman physiques and are wearing, half silver and half black, singlets.
The one on the left is wearing a pair of wrestling shoes with a pair of silver and black wrestling kick pads,covering his calves. He also has no facial hair and a slicked back, black undercut hair style.
The gentleman on the right is not wear shoes-because he wrestles better without them-and has black athletic tape around his ankles. He has a long black ponytail, with the sides shaved and a full black beard.
Also, had they not been sitting, you would be able to tell that both men are six feet, three inches tall.
The name of the gentleman on the left appears on the screen. And as he prepares to put black tape on his fist, he starts to speak.

Jacob Seone: So the Sixth Street Soldiers, want to go to war and show everyone that they tough?
They want everyone to think that they bad, cause they from the street?
Well boys, let me remind you, that we from the streets too!
Let me remind you how tough *we* are!
We've busted people open!
We've broken people's bodies!
We've sent people to the hospital!
And you boys wanna talk about being tough?

Description of Visual: *Jacob leans towards his partner and smiles. With the back of his hand, he taps his partner on the shoulder.*
As the bearded gentleman with the ponytail's name appears on the screen, he begins to loudly speak.

Joseph Leone: THE ONLY REASON WE AIN'T IN THE STREETS NO MORE, IS CAUSE WE LEFT THE STREET!
BUT SIXTH STREET SOLDIERS, JUST CAUSE WE AIN'T IN THE STREETS NO MORE, DON'T MEAN THE STREETS AIN'T STILL IN US! YOU CAN TALK TOUGH ALL YOU WANT! BUT EVERYONE KNOWS THAT TALK IS CHEAP!
YOU BOYS WANNA GO TO WAR? WELLTONIGHT, YOU GONNA FIND OUT THAT IT'S A BAD IDEA TO GO TO WAR… WITH A TITAN!

Description of Visual: *As the Titans start to put tape around their fist, we transition back to the arena.*
We see a sweeping shot of all the fans cheering with anticipation for the upcoming match.

Eric: After hearing those comments, you know it's going to be an epic contest!

Super Stud: Contest? Were you not listening? These two teams may be going to war, Eric!

Eric: Well whatever you call it, we don't have to wait because it's about to go down,!

Description of Visual: *While we continue to scan the crowd, we hear Ring Announcer, Tony Anderson, introduce the competitors of the match.*

Tony Anderson: Ladies and gentleman, this is our final match of the evening. It is a tag team contest. And it is scheduled for one fall.
The winning team will go on to face Trueno and Racha, Los Intensa Tormenta, next week.

Description of Visual: *The lights in the arena dim.*
An ominous military themed instrumental, begins playing.

Tony Anderson: Introducing first: they say that they hail from the toughest street in the world, Sixth Street. They weigh a combined weight of five hundred and twenty-five pounds. They are accompanied by Cali Ivey. Here are, Hagan Benally and Evan Skaggs, the Sixth Street Soldiers.

Description of Visuals: *Still wearing the same outfits we saw them in moments ago, the three members of the Sixth Street Soldiers, slowly walk out onto the stage. Hagan leading the way, followed by Evan and finally Cali.*
The three of them stop on the stage and position themselves side-by-side.
They slowly look around at the audience.
Then with three fingers raised on each hand, they cross their arm into an X across their chests.

Eric: The sign of the six is what they call that.

Super Stud: Yup. Everyone from Sixth Street does it?

Eric: So I've heard.

Super Stud: Well did you hear that if you're not from Sixth Street, you better not make the sign. False representation is punishable offense.

Eric: You're just full of Sixth Street facts.

Super Stud: I knew a girl from Sixth Street. Jennifer Ivey I believe her name was.

Eric: Jennifer Ivey? Isn't that Cali's mom?

Super Stud: Uh…let's just focus on the action, please!

Description of Visual: *While still making the sign of the six, the Sixth Street Soldiers start heading for the ring.*
The camera zooms in on Hagan's face. Despite not being heard throughout the arena, Hagan starts to do some trash talking to the people at home.
"Tonight, those Titan boys and everyone here, are gonna find out, that when you're from Sixth Street, you're better than everyone else.
Even though Hagan's comments weren't heard by anyone in the arena, everyone knows that Hagan said something arrogant.
There is a lot of contempt for not just Hagan, but all three members of the Sixth Street Soldiers and it can be heard all over the arena.
As Hagan walks passed the cameraman, Evan is next to appear in the shot. He too has a brief message for us.

"IT'S GONNA BE A BAD NIGHT FOR THE TITANS! A REAL BAD NIGHT!"
Evan then laughs manically as he heads to the ring.
We get one more close up shot, this time of Cali.
Cali doesn't say anything. She pushes the cameraman out of the way and continues to the ring.

Eric: Some pre-match words from the Sixth Street Soldiers.

Super Stud: It was actually just Hagan and Evan. Cali didn't have much to say.

Eric: Cali didn't have anything to say, actually.

Description of Visual: *All of three members of The Sixth Street Soldiers enter the ring.*
They walk to the center of the ring.
They once again arrogantly display the sign of the six.

Eric: You know, I've always wanted to ask you something, Stud.

Super Stud: What?

Eric: Have you ever been to Sixth Street?

Super Stud: Me? No way! I've heard too many bad stories about the place!

Eric: Any idea where it is?

Super Stud: I think it's in…

Description of Visual: *As Hagan and Evan head to their corner, an aggressive dirty south style rap beat, begins playing.*
Immediately, the fans jump to their feet and cheer the arrival of the next team.

Eric: It's amazing how much people have taken to these guys!

Tony Anderson: And their opponents, hail from San Francisco, California and weigh a combined weight of five hundred and sixty pounds. Here are Joseph Seone and Jacob Leone, the Titans of Tomorrow!

Description of Visual: *Joseph and Jacob walk out from with their heads down.*

They stop as they reach the edge of the stage and stand side-by-side, Jacob is on the right. Joseph is on the left.
Both men are taking a moment to absorb all the energy the crowd is giving them.

Eric: Jacob and Joseph making that one final shift to get ready for this encounter.

Super Stud: And once that shift is complete, no one is safe!

Description of Visual: *Jacob slowly raises his head and starts to loosen up his wrist*
Joseph snaps his head up and looks on, with a wild-eyed stare.

Eric: You can see it on their faces, these two men are now ready for battle!

Super Stud: They may be ready for battle, but are they better be ready for war!

Description of Visual: *The Titans start to stomp to ring.*
Jacob is leading the way, looking serious and focused.
Joseph is bringing up the rear, looking crazy. To add to Joseph's crazy, he begins to bark "TAU TAU TAU" prompting everyone in attendance to join in.

Eric: As usual, Joseph getting everyone to chant "fight" in Samoan.

Super Stud: I always thought he was just saying, hello or something.

Description of Visual: *Back in the ring, Hagan and Evan, have removed their vests and headgear, and are pacing in their corner, waiting for the Titans to arrive.*

Eric: This is sure to be an epic contest, Stud!

Super Stud: That's putting it mildly. Both of these teams have something to prove.

Description of Visual: *The Titans reach the ring.*
Joseph moves next to Jacob.
Both men simultaneously grab the second rope and pull themselves up onto the apron.

Eric: For those of you at home, if you've never seen a match with the Titans of Tomorrow, don't let their size fool you. Despite how big they are, they can do things that most men today can't do.

Super Stud: Hence the name Titans of Tomorrow.

Description of Visual: *The Titans enter the ring.*
Jacob walks to the corner to his left.
Joseph walks to the corner to his right.
Both men pull themselves onto the second set of ropes in their respective corner.
Jacob looks out into the crowd
Joseph keeps his head lowered.

Super Stud: I hate be a "back in my day" guy, but back in my day, there was a Samoan tag team that was just…well *wild*. But as great, and yes I said great, as those guys were, I never saw them do anything like Jacob and Joseph can do.

Eric: That's nice of you to say.

Super Stud: Well, I don't have a problem with Jacob or Joseph. So I'm not going to say anything bad about them.

Eric: You're scared of them aren't you?

Super Stud: No.
Maybe.
A little.
Let's move on.

Description of Visual: *While looking out at the crowd, Jacob runs his thumb under his neck.. He does this to symbolize that he and his partner intend on defeating their opponents.*
Joseph has his head down.
Suddenly, he snaps his head back, showing off a wild eyed look and extends his arms as well.

Eric: Make no mistake about it, these guys are ready.

Description of Visual: *We cut to a shot of The Sixth Street Soldiers, who are in their corner, talking strategy.*
Cali, is now on the apron, talking along with them.

Super Stud: A lot of people don't realize this, but Cali is a really good strategist.

Eric: Really?

Super Stud: Yeah. Hagan told me that a lot of the Sixth Street Soldiers' victories, can be credited to Cali's planning.

Description of Visual: *As The Titans music fades out, Jacob and Joseph drop down off the ropes.*
Joseph moves over to his team's designated corner, where Jacob is waiting.

Eric: I'm going to put you on the spot, Stud. Who do you think will take this match?

Super Stud: If what Hagan said about Cali is true, I'm going with the Sixth Street Soldiers.
I don't have a problem with the Titans, but they're on their own in this one.
Cali can give the Soldiers some insight from a different perspective.

Description of Visual: *After Joseph reaches Jacob, he looks towards the stage.*
There's a look of confusion on his face, as he looks at the stage.
Joseph's confusion bleeds over to Jacob, who is prompted to look at the stage as well.

Super Stud: What do you suppose is eating at the Titans?

Description of Visual: *After we cut to a shot of the stage, we see the AWO, Tag Team Champions, "The Jigga Man" Jamal Ryans and "Classy" Billy Foxx. The two of them are dressed in fancy attire with one of the World Tag Team championship belts, draped over their respective shoulders.*

Eric: Well we found out last week, that these guys have a new manager.

Super Stud: Yeah that Martin "The Intellect" guy.
I think hooking up with him has been really good for them. I mean this is the second week they've had on some nice clothes. Look at those white suits they have on. And those black loafers. And how about those sunglasses? Not to mention Billy Foxx has a nice ducktail style haircut and Jigga's got his hair nicely braided. Eric, you wish you looked as good as they do.

Eric: Well I don't know about that. But they do look pretty nice.

Description of Visual: *With everyone's eyes on them, the two men start walking towards the ring..*

Eric: You know, I actually forgot that Billy and Jamal had planned on coming out to watch this match.

Super Stud: Don't start, Eric! They didn't do anything last week so they're probably not going to do anything this week.

Eric: I'm not starting anything! I'm just saying I forgot they were coming!

Description of Visual: *Everyone in the ring now has their eyes on Billy and Jamal.*
When Billy and Jamal, reach the bottom of the ramp, they stop.
To ease everyone's minds, Jamal calmly motions to everyone in the ring, signifying that it's okay for them to start the match.

Eric: Glad to see we have Jamal's permission to get this contest underway.

Super Stud: I think Jamal is just saying that everyone needs to chill and stop trippin'.

Eric: Chill and stop trippin'?

Super Stud: Yeah. They need to cool out and be easy, blood.

Eric: I think *you* need to chill and be easy and stop trippin' before you hurt yourself.

Super Stud: You're just mad because *I'm* cooler than you.

Description of Visual: *Before Jacob and Joesph turn back to the ring, We hear Hagan yell, "HEY!" as he pushes the back of Jacob's head.*
Evan pushes the back of Joseph's head and he yells, "DON'T WORRY ABOUT THEM! YOU WORRY ABOUT US!"
Cali can be seen still on the apron, and can be heard yelling, "TELL'EM BOYS! TELL'EM!"

Super Stud: Oh boy.

Description of Visual: *Jacob and Joseph quickly turn around.*
As they look at Hagan and Evan, anger can be seen written all over their face.

Super Stud: The Sixth Street Soldiers, poking the bear. Or bears in this case.

Description of Visual: *Hagan and Evan taunt the Titans with the sign of the six.*
The Titans' temper starts to get the best of them, and they try to go after the
Soldiers.
The referee is able to get between the two teams and manages to convince them
to wait for the bell.

Eric: With all due respect to the referee, I think the only thing stopping the
Titans, is the fact that a title shot is on the line.

Super Stud: It's actually a shot at a shot. But I see what you mean.

Description of Visual: *The referee loudly orders that one man from each team*
leave the ring.

Eric: I gotta give this referee credit, he's not messing around with either team.

Description of Visual: *Evan leaves the ring, making the sign of the six as he*
exits.
Despite both he and Jacob still being angry, Joseph leaves the ring.
Hagan continues to taunt Jacob, and beckons for him to bring on the fight.
Jacob is visibly fuming. But before his temper completely boils over, the referee
quickly signals for the bell and the contest is officially under way.

<u>**Tag Team Match: The Titans of Tomorrow (Jacob Seone and Joseph**</u>
<u>**Leone) vs. The Sixth Street Soldiers (Hagan Benally and Evan Skaggs) w/**</u>
<u>**Cali Ivey in their corner**</u>

Eric: And here we go with this big time, tag team contest!

Description of Visual: *The referee moves out of the way, and allows the*
combatants to do battle.
Jacob swings wildly at Hagan with a clothesline.
Hagan is able to duck passed Jacob.

Super Stud: This one is starting off hot!

Description of Visual: *Joseph turns around.*
Hagan turns around as well. He quickly hits Jacob with a forearm strike to the jaw.

Eric: And Hagan with an impressive display of quickness.

Description of Visual: *Jacob is stunned by Hagan's forearm shot, but is still on his feet.*
Hagan quickly fires off another forearm shot, that stuns and staggers Jacob a little more.

Eric: Hagan may take Jacob off his feet.

Description of Visual: *Hagan decides to go for something different, and hits the ropes behind him.*
Hagan charges at Jacob.
Jacobs regains his wits and charges at Hagan.
Hagan has no time to react, as Jacob quickly extends his arm and knocks Hagan to the mat.

Eric: And a Jacob putting Hagan down with a wicked clothesline!

Description of Visual: *Hagan is hurt, but not enough to stay down. He manages to get to his feet and charges at Jacob.*
Before Hagan is able to attack, Jacob knocks him down with another clothesline.

Eric: Hagan taken down again!

Super Stud: But to his credit, he won't stay down!

Description of Visual: *Hagan gets to his feet one more time.*
Jacob runs him down with an even more powerful clothesline.

Eric: And it looks like Hagan is going to need a minute after that one!

Super Stud: Yeah Jacob really laid that one in! Hagan's lucky his head is still attached!

Description of Visual: *As Jacob beckons for Hagan to get up, the fans start to rally their support.*
Hagan does manage to get back to his feet, but he is so disoriented that he staggers over to a neutral corner.

Eric: Jacob has Hagan on the ropes!

Super Stud: Literally.

Description of Visual: *Jacob charges at Hagan.*
Hagan has no time to recover.
Jacob leaps into the air and hits Hagan with a back elbow strike.
After landing on his feet, Jacob can tell that Hagan is dazed and decides to quickly follows up his attack.
Jacob leaps and simultaneously turns in the air.
Jacob then kicks Hagan in the back of the head.

Eric: A back elbow followed by an enziguri from Jacob!

Super Stud: I don't know how a man of that size, can do a move like that!

Description of Visual: *As the fans once again cheer for Jacob, Hagan drops to one knee, before collapsing face first to the mat.*
Jacob is about to go for a pin, but Hagan manages to retreat to the floor.

Eric: Hagan taking an early timeout in this contest.

Super Stud: Sometimes you have to reset, reevaluate and re...approach.

Eric: You struggled with that last one, huh?

Super Stud: I struggle with looking at your face every week.

Description of Visual: *Hagan staggers away from the ring a bit and almost bumps into Billy and Jamal. He is unsure who is near him and quickly raises his fist, ready to fight.*

Eric: And Hagan about to get into it with The…M.V.T.'s I believe they're now calling themselves.

Super Stud: That's right. The Most Valuable Tag Team.

Eric: Shouldn't it be M.V.T.T.'s?

Super Stud: No! One "T" is fine!

Description of Visual: *Billy and Jamal raise their hands, signifying that they do not want any problems.*
Before Hagan can start a fight with the tag team champions, Evan and Cali run over to him.
Evan and Cali grab Hagan by the shoulders, and pull him away.

Eric: I'd say that's a smart move on Evan and Cali's part.

Super Stud: Yeah, definitely. No need to start something that doesn't need to be started.

Description of Visual: *The Sixth Street Soldiers head up the aisle way a bit, in order to put some space between themselves and the Titans and go over some strategy.*
As the three of them talk, Cali sees the cameraman.
To wanting to be disturbed, Cali yells at the cameraman to "BEAT IT!" before pushing him away by the lens

Super Stud: I don't think Cali likes having cameras in her face.

Eric: I think you're right.
He better be careful too. Cali is not above hitting anyone, whether they're holding a camera or not.

Description of Visual: *Back in the ring, the referee is demanding that Hagan get back into the contest and that Evan get back into his corner.*
The Soldiers begin heading towards the ring, when Evan barks at the referee to stop telling them what to do.
Cali chimes in and tells the referee to back off.
As the Soldiers yell at the referee on the outside of the ring, Jacob is still in the ring, beckoning for them to bring on the fight.
The referee decides not to argue any longer and begins his standard ten-count.

Eric: This must be part of that *"re-approach"* you talked about.

Super Stud: You try so hard to be witty. But…you're not very good at it.

Description of Visual: *The referee's count reaches three, just as Hagan climbs up onto the apron.*
Evan climbs up as well and he and Hagan whisper some last minute strategy.
Jacob is still in the center of the ring, rubbing his hands together and eagerly waiting for Hagan.
The referee motions for Hagan to get in the ring and rejoin the contest.
Hagan sneers at the referee and dismissively waves him away.

Eric: Hagan not in much of a hurry to rejoin the match.

Super Stud: That's smart. He's slowing the pace down and making Jacob wrestle at his speed.

Description of Visual: *Hagan finally re-enters the ring.*
The referee once again motions for Hagan to get back into the match.
Hagan slowly starts walking toward Jacob.
Suddenly, Hagan looks at the referee and frowns.

Super Stud: Looks like Hagan is tired of dealing with the referee's lip.

Description of Visual: *Hagan points his finger in the referee's direction.*

Eric: It looks like Hagan's about to give the referee a mouthful.

Description of Visual: *Hagan quickly charges at Jacob*
Jacob is not prepared for this and Hagan, drives the sole of his boot into Jacob's gut.

Eric: And Hagan with the fake out on Jacob!

Super Stud: Classic! Make'em think you're going right and then go left! I love it!

Description of Visual: *Jacob grabs his stomach and staggers backwards a bit.*
Hagan quickly follows Jacob in and hurts him with a clubbing forearm shot to the back.

Super Stud: As thick as Jacob is, Hagan had to be putting some real power behind that shot.

Description of Visual: *Hagan delivers another powerful clubbing shot to Jacob's back.*
Jacob's body stiffens up, and he staggers backward even farther away from Hagan.
Jacob ends up in the neutral corner behind him.
Hagan quickly follows Jacob and delivers a punch to his stomach.

Eric: Get him out of the corner, ref!

Super Stud: Let the ref do his job, Eric!

Description of Visual: *Hagan drives another punch into Jacob's gut.*
The referee orders Hagan to back away.
Hagan looks at the referee with anger in his eyes.

Super Stud: If looks could kill, that referee would be a goner.

Description of Visual: *While he is not happy about it, Hagan listens to the referee and backs away to the center of the ring.*
Despite following the referee's orders, Hagan once again points at the referee and demands that he stop telling him what to do.

Super Stud: All right ref, get off Hagan's back!

Eric: What happened to *"let the ref do his job"*?

Super Stud: I am letting him do his job! But he needs to calm down and get off of Hagan's back!

Description of Visual: *Hagan refocuses on Jacob.*
Jacob is in the corner, doubled over, holding his stomach.
Hagan charges at Jacob.
To everyone's surprise, Jacob charges out of the corner.
In one fluid motion, Jacob places his right arm between Hagan's legs, and reaches over Hagan's shoulder with his left arm.
Then, Jacob spins over, while keeping Hagan horizontal across his body, and drives him into the mat.

Eric: And a scoop powerslam out of nowhere by Jacob!

Super Stud: You are really underselling how impressive that was!

Do you understand the skill it takes to run at someone, grab them, lift them up and then spin and slam them to the ground?
Everytime I've seen him do that, it impresses me! And I don't impress easily!

Description of Visual: *Jacob stays on top of Hagan for a lateral press style pin.*
The referee gets in position.
He hits the mat once.
He strikes it a second time.
But the count stops when Evan quickly sneaks into the ring, and strikes Jacob in the back with a clubbing forearm smash.

Eric: And Evan in to break up the pin!

Super Stud: Smart move too! That may have been it!

Description of Visual: *Evan prepares to hit Jacob again.*
Joseph quickly enters the ring and goes after Evan.
Evan doesn't see it coming, but Joseph pushes him away from Jacob.
After gathering his footing, Evan pushes Joseph back.
Joseph starts to beckon for Evan to bring on the fight.
The referee steps in between the two and stops them from exchanging blows.

Eric: This contest is really heating up!

Super Stud: Yeah it is!
I think a shot at those tag titles is the only thing keeping this match, somewhat civil!

Description of Visual: *Despite being still full of anger, both Joseph and Evan follow the referee's demands and leave the ring.*
After Joseph storms out onto the apron, he extends his hand and screams out to Jacob, "TAG ME IN, NOW!"

Eric: Joseph really wants in this match!

Super Stud: Really? What was your first clue?

Description of Visual: *Evan is on the apron, stomping his foot on the mat like a maniac.*
Hagan manages to get to his hands and knees and starts to crawl towards Evan.
Evan aggressively extends hand and looks at Joseph.

Evans Screams at Hagan , in a very intimidating fashion, "I'M GONNA MESS YOU UP PUNK!"

Super Stud: Boy, Joseph and Evan are like two caged dogs ready to fight!

Eric: Everyone knows that they are the ones on their respective teams, with the fiery tempers.

Description of Visual: *The anticipation to see these two men go at it, is really high.*
Jacob gets back to his feet and slowly makes his way over to Joseph.
The arena erupts with cheers when Jacob and Hagan, simultaneously tag their partners.

Eric: Hagan and Joseph are now the legal men for their teams.

Description of Visual: *The two men enter the ring quickly.*
They charge towards each other.
They both have the same idea and try to knock each other down with shoulder blocks.
To everyone's surprise, neither man budges.

Super Stud: Whoa. The unmoving force of nature meets the unmovable dense object, as they say.

Eric: That's not quite how *they* say it, actually.

Super Stud: Well you know what I mean!

Description of Visual: *Joseph and Evan stare at each other, with fire in their eyes.*
The tension in the arena is high.
Suddenly, Evan strikes Joseph with a closed fist punch to the jaw.

Super Stud: Well that wasn't legal, but it was effective.   .

Description of Visual: *Joesph staggers backwards and tries to regain his composure.*
The referee warns Evan about using a closed fist.
As he warns Evan, Joseph touches his jaw and looks out at the fans.
The fans rally behind Joseph and begin chanting, "Tau! Tau! Tau!"

The cheers seem to motivate Joseph.
Joseph looks back at Evan and retaliates with a closed fist punch to the jaw, of his own.

Eric: And Joseph showing he can not only take a punch, but deliver one as well.

Description of Visual: *The referee steps in and warns both Evan and Joseph about closed fist punching*

Eric: That's probably the first and last warning those two will receive.

Super Stud: So if they both get disqualified, I guess Los Intensa Tormenta will get the title shot?

Eric: I believe so.

Super Stud: I practiced saying their name all week and you're not going to say anything?

Eric: OH YEAH! YOU DID SAY IT RIGHT!

Description of Visual: *Neither Evan nor Joseph want to get disqualified, but they are still filled with anger.*
Evan begins flexing and grunting at Joseph.
Joseph extends his arms, and lets out a ferocious yell.

Eric: I think that Samoan wild side has woken up.

Super Stud: I don't think it ever sleeps, Eric.

Description of Visual: *Joseph hits the ropes behind him.*
He runs back at Evan.
Evan swings his arm wildly at Joseph...

Eric: Clothesline attempt by Evan.

Description of Visual: *...but Joseph lowers his head to avoid it.*

Eric: Joseph ducks out of the way.

Description of Visual: *Joseph runs passed Evan and hits the parallel set of ropes.*
He rebounds off of those ropes.
Just as Evan turns around, Joseph leaps at him and knocks him to the mat with a clothesline.

Eric: And Evan taken off his feet in a major way!

Description of Visual: *The fans in the arena go crazy.*
Evan tries to collect himself, while Joseph looks down on him and aggressively beckons for him to get back on his feet.

Eric: And Joseph showing Evan, why you don't go to war with a Titan!

Description of Visual: *Evan refuses to stay down and manages to pull himself up to his knees.*
Joseph wraps his arm around Evan's head and pulls him to his feet.
Evan is having a tough time defending himself, and Joseph easily drags him over to he and Jacob's corner.

Eric: Joseph has Evan trapped in a front face lock and is taking him to "Titan Town."

Super Stud: Titan Town? Did you really just say that?

Eric: I did.
And I realized how bad that was, after I said it.

Description of Visual: *Jacob slaps Joseph on the back, tagging himself into the match.*

Eric: Jacob now the legal man.

Description of Visual: *Jacob enters the ring.*
Joseph still has Evan trapped, while Jacob climbs onto the second rope.
Joseph moves away from the corner a little.

Eric: Evan now in trouble.

Description of Visual: *Joseph scoops up Evan and with a lot of power.*
Evan collides with the mat, after Joseph bodyslams him to the mat.

As Evan's body hits the mat, Jacob leaps off the second rope and lands back first onto Evans chest.

Eric: And a second rope, senton splash by Jacob!

Description of Visual: *As Joseph is leaving the ring, Hagan illegally re-enters the ring.*
Hagan charges at Jacob but Jacob quickly gets to his feet.
Before Hagan can attack, Jacob grabs Hagan around the waist, pivots and slams him back first onto Evan.

Eric: And now Jacob belly-to-belly suplexing Hagan *onto* Evan!

Super Stud: You can't use someone's partner as a weapon against them!

Description of Visual: *The fan loudly vocalize their support for Jacob, as he quickly gets back to his feet.*
Jacob is so fired up that he lets out yell and begins pounding his chest.

Eric: And once again the fans are showing their love for the Titans of Tomorrow!

Super Stud: He should be trying to win and not showing off for these idiots in the audience!

Eric: They're not idiots! They're showing their support to one of their favorites!

Super Stud: Well anyone that would cheer someone who isn't smart enough to go for the win, is an idiot in my book!

Description of Visual: *As the fans settle back down, Hagan slowly rolls off of Evan.*
Hagan slides under the bottom rope, until he reaches the floor.
Evan starts to slowly get to his feet
Jacob heads over to Evan.

Eric: Jacob getting back on the attack.

Super Stud: He should have stayed on the attack, if you ask me!

Eric: Well we didn't ask you, but thanks anyway.

Super Stud: You ain't too old to get whooped, Eric! And I ain't to old to whoop you!

Description of Visual: *Jacob grabs Evan by the head and pulls him to his feet.*
He pulls Evan over to he and Joseph's corner.
Evan is still a little dazed and Jacob slams his head into the turnbuckle.

Super Stud: You know, a lot of these…*fans* don't appreciate how much having your head slammed into the turnbuckle hurts! They seems to think that the padding protects you or something!
Well just imagine, tripping and falling and landing head first into the arm of your couch. Then, come talk to me about it!

Eric: Thank you for that analysis, Stud.

Description of Visual: *Evan collapses to one knee.*
Jacob prepares to follow up on his attack, but catches sight of the tag team champs, strolling over to the Titans side of the ring.

Eric: Classy and The Jigga-Man on the…

Super Stud: If you start making a big deal about them being on the move, I'm going to…

Eric: I wasn't going to make a big deal about it! I was just going to say that they were on the move possibly trying to get a better view of things.

Description of Visual: *Jacob returns his attention to Evan. He grabs him by the side of the head and pulls him back to his feet.*
Jacob is about to hit Evan with a forearm, when Cali jumps up on the apron.

Eric: Cali better be careful or she's going to get her team disqualified!

Super Stud: And the way Jack is, she could possibly even get fined.

Description of Visual: *Cali starts to yell at the referee, demanding that he make Jacob get off of Evan.*

Super Stud: Cali does have a point. Evan is in the ropes. So The referee should make Jacob move.

Eric: True. But before he can address Jacob, Cali needs to get off the apron.

Super Stud: You're just taking up for The Titans, cause you're a Titan fan.

Eric: You're the one who's scared of them.

Super Stud: I'm not scared of them! I just have a healthy respect for them!

Description of Visual: *Cali gives in to the referee's demands, and gets to the floor.*
While on the floor, Cali continues to argue with the referee, which starts to anger and distract Joseph.

Eric: Cali really needs to get out of here!

Super Stud: You make her leave!

Description of Visual: *Both Joseph and the referee are yelling at Cali.*
Cali's distraction allows Hagan to reach into the ring under the bottom rope and grab Jacob by the ankle.
Joseph sees this and is furiously drops off the apron.

Eric: Joseph not going to stand for this!

Description of Visual: *Joseph goes after Hagan and Cali.*
Hagan releases Jacob's ankle and is prepared to fight it out with Joseph.

Eric: The referee needs to get some control! This thing is getting out of hand!

Description of Visual: *The referee quickly jumps to the floor and prevents Joseph and Hagan from fighting.*
Back in the ring, Jacob is finally able to focus on Evan.
The distraction gave Evan enough time to regain his wits. He reaches back and delivers a closed-fist punch square to Jacob's jaw.

Eric: Now he was warned about that! That should have been a disqualification, Stud! How is that right?

Super Stud: Simple, he used his right hand.

Eric: Really?

Super Stud: Yeah! And he put a lot more power behind it too! A whole lot of power!

Eric: Wow, Stud.

Super Stud: Wow indeed, Eric! I was impressed by that punch too!

Description of Visual: *Jacob staggers backwards before collapsing to one knee.*

Super Stud: To be fair, I think Jacob being caught off guard, played a part in why the punch had a bigger impact this time.

Description of Visual: *Joseph sees Jacob in trouble. He's not sure what happened, but he knows that Evan did something illegal.*

Super Stud: Joseph looks like he's about to do something. The referee better stop him referee!

Eric: What?

Super Stud: What do you mean what? Joseph can't get in the ring! He's not the legal man!

Eric: But a closed-fist punch is legal?

Super Stud: You never heard me say that, did you?

Description of Visual: *Joseph quickly slides into the ring and tries to go after Evan.*
The referee quickly goes after Joseph and stops him.
This leads to an argument between the referee and Joseph.

Eric: This referee is working over time! We might need two referees for this match!

Description of Visual: *As Joseph and the referee argue, Hagan sneaks into the*

ring.
While Evan continues to recover, Hagan extends his arm and quickly hits Jacob between the neck and chest.

Eric: And Hagan taking advantage of the referee being distracted by Joseph.

Super Stud: Hagan also took Joseph down with a clothesline.

Description of Visual: *Evan stays on Jacob and starts laying in stomps to his body.*

Super Stud: As good as they are, the one thing that hurts The Titans, is their fiery tempers.

Description of Visual: *After getting in a few more stomps, Hagan quickly sneaks out of the ring.*
Evan has been given enough time to recover, and goes in for the attack.
Jacob is unable to defend himself Evan's barrage of forearms.

Super Stud: It's no secret that the Titans can take a beating. Staying on the attack is the smart thing to do.

Description of Visual: *Evan gets to his feet and begins to beats on his chest. He also let's out a roar that clearly shows that he is fired up and back in the fight. Despite the beating he has taken, Jacob tries to sit up. Unfortunately, his body will not allow it.*

Super Stud: And Look at that, Eric. It just goes to show that if you chop at a tree long enough, it will eventually fall!

Description of Visual: *Joseph begrudgingly gives in and leaves the ring.*
The referee's attention returns to the match, just as Evan is going for the pin.
The referee gets into position.
There's a one count.
There's a two count.
Before the three, Jacob quickly gets his shoulder off the mat.

Eric: And a two count by the referee.

Description of Visual: *After getting his shoulder off the mat, Jacob manages to roll onto his stomach.*

Evan believes that Jacob is going to try and crawl over to his partner, and quickly gets in front of him.
Evan leaps into the air.
As he lands, Evan stomps on Jacob's upper back.

Super Stud: There you go Evan, get him!

Description of Visual: *Jacob grimaces in pain as he clutches at the point of of Evan's impact.*
Evan starts to feel a little cocky. He stands back watches as Jacob slowly and painfully, pulls himself back to his feet.

Super Stud: Hmm.

Eric: What?

Super Stud: I'm not sure I agree with this. I'll have to wait and see how it plays out.

Description of Visual: *Despite being back on his feet, Jacob so hurt and disoriented, that he staggers into the Sixth Street Soldiers corner.*

Eric: Jacob is really in trouble now.

Super Stud: Yes he is! He's about to find out what it was like growing up on Sixth Street.

Description of Visual: *Evan reaches Jacob, and grabs him by the hair.*
Evan quickly starts peppering Jacob with alternating forearms to the jaw.
Jacob tries his best to defend himself, but collapses into the corner.

Eric: Evan with a real showing of dominance at the moment.

Super Stud: He's what I like to call, a mauler, Eric. That's an old school term by the way.

Eric: I assumed that it was, Stud.

Description of Visual: *Jacob is down in the corner, with his back against the bottom turnbuckle.*
The referee orders Evan to back away from Jacob, but Evan does not listen.

Evan instead, starts driving his foot, into Jacob's chest, in order to keep him grounded.

Eric: And just look at this! Evan is just grinding Jacob into the ground!

Super Stud: Yes he is! He's grinding him like a used cigarette!

Description of Visual: *Evan continues grinding away, as the referee starts his count.*
We hear the referee's count 1-2-3-4
Evan backs away from Jacob before the count reaches 5.

Eric: Evan cutting it close with that one.

Description of Visual: *Evan scowls at the referee and raises his fist, in a threatening fashion..*

Super Stud: No-no, Evan, don't do that! He might deserve it, but you don't want to get disqualified!

Eric: So you're telling me, that the referee deserves to get punched because he's doing his job?

Super Stud: No. He deserves to get punched because he's *not* doing his job correctly. The cadence of his count is way too fast.

Description of Visual: *The referee gets in front of Evan and the two of them begin to argue.*
The referee reminds Evan who the authority figure in the match is.
Evan reminds the referee why he doesn't care.
As this is going on, Hagan quickly enters the ring and starts stomping on Jacob's chest.

Eric: Look, I'm not going to deny how tough the Sixth Street Soldiers are, but why do they have to cheat?

Super Stud: It's only cheating if the referee catches them.

Description of Visual: *Joseph quickly enters the ring.*
After whizzing past Evan and the referee's argument, he pulls Hagan off of his partner.

Hagan tries to retaliate, but the referee sees what is happening and steps in between them.
The referee orders both men to stop fighting and go back onto the apron, in their respective corners.

Eric: I can't believe how much tension there is between these two teams!

Super Stud: It's a street thing. Both teams want the titles, but they also want to be called, the toughest.

Description of Visual:*Hagan and Joseph don't listen to the referee so the referee once again demands both Hagan and Joseph to leave the ring.*
This time, the referee adds the warning, that if they don't leave the ring now, he will disqualify both teams.
The two men leave the ring but the bickering between them continues.

Eric: And look! With all the excitement, I almost didn't notice what Evan was doing behind the referee's back!

Description of Visual: *As Hagan, Joseph and the referee were having their interaction, Evan was in the corner, driving his foot into Jacob's neck.*

Super Stud: The referee didn't tell him to stop, so he's not breaking any rules!

Eric: As long as it makes sense to you, right?

Description of Visual: *Evan sets Jacob free, just before the referee sees what he was doing.*
With Hagan back on the apron, Evan tags him back into the match.

Eric: Hagan now the legal man for his team.

Description of Visual: *Jacob grabs the top rope and tries to get to his feet. Evan quickly stomps on his chest, in order to keep him grounded.*

Eric: Evan getting in another stomp for good measure.

Super Stud: You gotta use a period when you're making statement.

Eric: I think I get what you're trying to say.

Super Stud: Just go with it!

Description of Visual: *Hagan and Evan make their way, over to the neutral corner, that is parallel from their current position.*

Eric: Double team maneuver coming up.

Description of Visual: *Evan grabs Hagan by the wrist and flings him towards Jacob.*

Eric: Evan Irish whipping his partner out of the corner.

Description of Visual:*Just before Hagan reaches Jacob, he flips forward and crashes back first into Jacob.*

Eric: And flipping senton into the corner!

Description of Visual: *While Hagan is moving out of the way, Evan runs towards Jacob.*
To everyone's surprise, Evan performs a flipping senton into Jacob of his own.

Super Stud: Wow! The Titans aren't the only big men that can do
some…flipping amazing stuff!
Get it?

Eric: You're right Stud, that was amazing!
And yeah, I got it. It wasn't funny, but I got it.

Super Stud: Oh what do you know about comedy, anyway? You thought puns
were something you kept in the kitchen with the pots.

Description of Visual: *Evan and Hagan get back to their feet and make the sign
of the six.*
The two men start to parade around the ring and loudly proclaim to the world,
"NO ONE IS TOUGHER THAN US!"

Super Stud: Guys, get the victory first! Then tell everyone how tough you are!

Description of Visual: *While still making their sign, Evan and Hagan look at
Joseph, and scream,* "YOU GUYS AIN'T SO TOUGH!"
Joseph starts to enter the ring, but knows it would be a bad idea.

Eric: Joseph is practicing great restraint, not going after the soldiers.

Description of Visual: *The referee demands that Evan leave the ring. As Evan heads to the corner, he yells at the referee, "THEY AIN'T SO TOUGH!"*

Eric: It's fascinating to me how determined The Soldiers are, to let everyone know that the Titans aren't tough.

Super Stud: As they say, "Gotta let'em know."

Eric: I'm sorry, who says that?

Super Stud: I heard it in a rap song.

Description of Visual: *Jacob tries to get back to his feet. He is hurting but he is taking advantage of every second that Hagan and Evan showboat.*

Super Stud: Something else Hagan and Evan need to think about, is that all that time they spend playing, is giving Jacob time to recover. That's why I keep stressing for teams to stay on their opponents.

Description of Visual: *While Evan is leaving the ring, Hagan grabs Jacob by the ankles and drags him out of the corner.*

Eric: Jacob being set up for something.

Description of Visual: *Still holding onto Jacob's ankles, Hagan looks down on Jacob. The referee watches closes as Hagan stomps on Jacob's lower stomach.*

Eric: You know, one inch lower and that would have been a disqualification.

Super Stud: One inch lower and Jacob would be crying and talking in a higher octave.

Description of Visual: *Jacob painfully grabs at his stomach and rolls onto his side. Hagan quickly moves to Jacob's head.*

He leaps into the air.
As Hagan comes in for a sideways landing, he drives his fist into Jacob's head.

Super Stud: This is how tag team wrestling should be done. You cut the ring in half, so to speak. You combine attacks. And you stay on your opponents.

Eric: Did you ever have a tag team partner, Stud?

Super Stud: Yeah. But it never worked out cause they were all too arrogant and had really bad attitudes.

Eric: I see.

Description of Visual: *Hagan quickly pulls Jacob onto his back.*
He presses Jacob's shoulders to the mat and goes for the pin.

Eric: Hagan trying to go for the win!

Description of Visual: *The referee gets down into position.*
He hits the mat once.
Then the referee hits the mat twice.
But Jacob pops his shoulder off the mat before the three.

Super Stud: Now don't let up! Stay on him!

Eric: You're really rooting for those guys aren't you?

Super Stud: I feel like I can relate to them. I think it's because I grew up in the streets just like they did.

Eric: Oh.

Description of Visual: *Hagan quickly...*

Eric: Wait a minute! No you didn't! You grew up in Beverly Hills!

Super Stud: Well yeah! But it was the west side of Beverly Hills!

Description of Visual: *Hagan quickly gets to his feet.*
His anger is on full display as he starts aggressively stomping onto Jacob's

upper body.

Super Stud: See that? That's smart. Jacob can't be a threat, if he's not on his feet.

Description of Visual: *Following the stomps, Hagan quickly travels to his corner and tags Evan back into the match.*

Eric: Evan once again the legal man of the match.

Description of Visual: *While Hagan is leaving the ring and Evan is entering, Jacob manages to roll over onto his stomach.*
He forces himself onto his hands and knees.
Before he can make any moves, Evan gets in front of Jacob and grabs him by the hair.
Evan then pulls Jacob, until he is back on his feet.

Super Stud: If they continue to stay on Jacob, this match will probably be over soon.

Description of Visual: *Evan looks at Hagan and nods.*
Hagan drapes his knee on the middle rope.
Once he's in position, Hagan nods back at Evan.

Super Stud: Did you see that? That's the mark of a *great* team, Eric! When you don't have to verbalize with each other? That's next level stuff right there!

Description of Visual: *Evan drags Jacob over to Hagan.*
He rears Jacob back.
He slams Jacob's head into Hagan's knee.

Super Stud: Nice double teaming by The Soldiers!

Eric: I wouldn't classify that as nice.

Super Stud: Oh quit griping! At least Hagan was still on the apron!

Description of Visual: *Jacob is on spaghetti legs.*
Evan holds onto Jacob's hair and keeps him from falling.
Hagan extends his hand.
Evan tags Hagan back into the match.

Eric: Tag made. Hagan is now the legal man.

Description of Visual: *Hagan enters the ring.*
Evan forces Jacob back into he and Hagan's corner.
Jacob is still disoriented and is draped, chest first against the turnbuckle.
Both members of the Sixth Street Soldiers hurry to the center of the ring.

Super Stud: I love it when they do this!

Description of Visual: *Hagan grabs Evan by the wrist.*
He Irish whips Evan towards Jacob.
Just as Evan closes in on Jacob, he ducks down and viciously rams his shoulder into Jacob's ribs.

Eric: And a shoulder block by Evan to Jacob!

Super Stud: He could have broken a rib with that!

Description of Visual: *Jacob clutches at his ribs, as he staggers backwards out of the corner. Despite the pain, Jacob wills himself not to drop to one knee.*

Eric: Jacob is in serious trouble.

Super Stud: He looks like he's about to puke!

Description of Visual: *Evan and Hagan position themselves behind Jacob, on opposite sides. Evan is on Jacob's left and Hagan on Jacob's right.*
Both Sixth Street Soldiers tuck their heads under Jacob's respective arms.
They lift Jacob up onto their shoulder.
They fall backwards and drop Jacob onto his back.

Eric: And a double back suplex by The Sixth Street Soldiers!

Super Stud: Impressive! You can't deny how well these two work together!

Description of Visual: *As Evan leaves the ring, Hagan prepares to go for the pin.*
Suddenly, Hagan is distracted, when he sees Billy approaching Cali.

Eric: Now what's going on here?

Super Stud: They've been so well-behaved I forgot the M.V.T.'s   were out there.
Anyway, the way Billy's smiling, I believe it's a case of a shooter, shooting his shot.

Eric: A what?

Super Stud: Just watch.

Description of Visual: *As Billy closes in on Cali, he reaches into his pocket.*
Billy smiles, as he pulls out a card.
When he reaches Cali, he hands her the card.
Surprisingly, Cali takes the card, and smiles back at Billy.
Billy then puts his thumb to his ear and his pinky to his mouth, signifying a phone and mouths the words, "call me."

Super Stud: Yup. That was definitely a shooter, shooting his shot.

Eric: Well whatever you call it these days, I don't know if Cali's going for it or not.

Description of Visual: *Before Cali can respond, we hear Hagan yell, "Hey get away from her!"*

Eric: Hagan isn't having any of Billy flirting or "*shooting*" with Cali.

Super Stud: Sixth Street sticks together.

Description of Visual: *Billy raises his hands and slowly backs away from Cali.*
He gives Cali a wink for good measure,
He turns and starts to walk away.

Eric: Well that was…interesting.

Super Stud: Yeah. Billy could teach you a thing or two about being smooth, Eric.

Eric: You know I'm a happily married man, Stud.

Super Stud: Yeah but is your wife happily married?

Description of Visual: *Cali's eyes lock on Hagan. She appears unsure of what to say.*
When the fans begin chanting Tau! Tau! Tau!*, Cali's expression changes.*
Cali realizes that Hagan needs get his head back in the game and she yell at him to, "worry about the match and not me!"

Eric: Cali's laying down the law, right about now.

Super Stud: As she should! You can talk about personal business after the match!

Description of Visual: *Hagan's emotions of both anger and confusion, are clearly displayed on his face. Despite how he feels, Hagan aggressively turns away from Cali.*
While Hagan's back was turned, Cali puts the card in her sports bra.

Super Stud: I guess it's safe to say that Billy shot and scored on this one.

Eric: Well he shot, but he hasn't scored yet.

Super Stud: I…touchè.

Description of Visual: *While Hagan was distracted by Cali and Billy, Jacob had time to roll onto his stomach and start crawling towards his partner.*

Eric: Hagan better get to Jacob before Jacob reaches Joseph!

Super Stud: A fresh and rested Joseph is a dangerous Joseph.

Description of Visual: *The "race" is on. Jacob is closing in on Joseph and Hagan is closing in on Jacob.*
The fans wait with baited breath, to see who will accomplish their goal.
Both Jacob and Joseph have their hands extended and are inches away from touching.
To the dismay of everyone, Hagan grabs Joseph by the ankle. and pulls him away from Jacob.

Eric: And Hagan able to put a stop to Jacob's progression.

Description of Visual: *Hagan quickly gets in front of Jacob,
He grabs him by the hair.*

Super Stud: I guess Jacob is going back to Sixth Street.

Description of Visual: *Hagan forces Jacob's head down.
With Jacob bent over, Hagan raises his arm and delivers a strong clubbing
forearm shot to Jacob's spine.*

Super Stud: Oof! He really laid that one in!

Description of Visual: *Jacob let out a loud scream. The scream did not come
off as a scream of pain, but as if a bolt of anger shot through his body.*

Eric: That sounded…

Super Stud: Guttural?

Eric: Yeah, that's a good word.

Description of Visual: *Jacob slowly stands up and looks at Hagan.
Hagan looks back at Jacob concerned.
Before Hagan can react, Jacob strikes him with a massive forearm to the jaw.*

Eric: And Jacob not ready to die just yet!

Description of Visual: *Hagan staggers backwards before dropping to one knee.*

Eric: That shot really rocked Hagan!

Description of Visual: *Jacob tries to move, but the surge of energy he
experienced, seems to have expired, and he too drops to one knee.*

Eric: Can you believe the match we've seen, so far?

Super Stud: It's incredible, Eric!

Description of Visual: *Hagan manages to pull himself up. He knows that he
needs to get the drop on Jacob.*

Hagan hits the ropes behind him.
He rebounds and runs towards Jacob.
Before Hagan is able to attack, Jacob sees Hagan and leg sweeps him, causing
him to fall face first to the mat.

Super Stud: And that was not a traditional leg sweep,Eric! Jacob swung his leg
counter clockwise and hit Hagan in the front of the legs! Unlike traditionally,
where you swing your leg clockwise and hit the person from the back of the leg!

Description of Visual: *Hagan lays on the mat clutching at his lips and nose and*
trying to massage away the pain.
Meanwhile, Jacob is on his hands and knees, trying to muster up the strength to
start crawling over to Joseph.

Eric: Both Joseph and Hagan are down once again!

Super Stud: And they both need to reach their partners!

Description of Visual: *Out on the apron, Evan and Joseph are throwing out*
their own form of encouragement, from their respective corners.
Evan is loudly demanding for Hagan to get up, while Joseph is clapping and
beckoning for his partner to make the tag.
Joseph is not the only one encouraging Jacob, the fans are encouraging Jacob
as well.
The arena is full of people stomping and loudly chanting Tau-Tau-Tau.

Eric: The crowd is really getting into this one, Stud!

Super Stud: Yeah, but is it going to do Jacob any good?

Description of Visual: *While still holding his face, Hagan manages to get to*
one knee. He knows that he needs to get to his partner, but the pain in his face,
as well as a little bit of dizziness, is making it difficult.
Jacob on the other hand, has started to crawl towards Joseph and is getting
closer and closer.

Eric: Who's going to make it to their partner first, Stud?

Super Stud: At this rate, I'm going to say, Jacob. Hagan better get a move on!

Description of Visual: *As Jacob is continuing to make progress, Hagan is able*

to push himself back to his feet. His balance is off and struggles to get his footing.
After managing to orient himself. Hagan is able to find and reach Evan and tag him into the match.

Eric: Evan now the legal man in the match.

Super Stud: I guess I was wrong.

Description of Visual: *While Evan is trying to enter the ring, Hagan is still a little out of it. Because of this, Hagan bumps into Evan, preventing him from entering the ring.*
The little collision gives Jacob more time to get closer to Joseph.

Super Stud: What are they doing? They're getting in each others way!

Description of Visual: *The Sixth Street Soldiers, manage to get themselves together and Evan is able to finally enter the ring.*
Tension engulfs the arena as Evan quickly goes after Jacob.

Eric: Jacob better hurry!

Super Stud: Evan better hurry!

Description of Visual: *Jacob manages to get to his feet, and he begins to take a step.*
Evan closes in on him and raises his arm.
Evan knows he needs to stop Jacob and clubs him in the back.
Evan thinks that the shot is going to knock Jacob down. Instead, it causes Jacob to stumble forward and allows him to slap Joseph's hand, just before he collapses to the mat.   .

Eric: And Jacob makes the tag! Joseph is now the legal man!

Description of Visual: *As Jacob rolls out of the ring, a large burst of elation , explodes in the arena.*
Evan is visibly angry, at the mistake he made. He quickly tries to rectify his error, by trying to get the drop on Joseph, who is still on the apron.
Evan tries to strike Joseph with a wild forearm. Joseph quickly grabs the middle rope, ducks down and drives his shoulder into Evan's stomach.

Eric: And Joseph is ready for battle!

Description of Visual: *Evan clutches at his abdomen as he slowly backs away from the ropes.*
Joseph quickly enters the ring and immediately goes on the attack.

Super Stud: Evan better be ready to defend himself!

Description of Visual: *When Joseph reaches Evan, he hits him in the jaw with a forearm.*

Eric: And Evan sent to the mat!

Super Stud: Yeah but he's getting back up!

Description of Visual: *As soon as Evan is on his feet, Joseph knocks him back to mat with another forearm to the jaw.*
Evan quickly gets back to his feet, once more.
Joseph spins to build up momentum, before sending Evan crashing to the mat with a powerful forearm to the jaw.

Eric: And Joseph is fired up and ready to go!

Description of Visual: *The fans are going insane.*
Evan quickly crawls away from Jacob, but Jacob is in hot pursuit.
Evan reaches the ropes.
He pulls himself to his feet.
He turns around.
Joseph waste no time and drives his foot into Evan stomach.

Eric: Evan is doubled over in pain!

Super Stud: Hey come on ref! Evan's in the ropes!

Description of Visual: *The referee demands that Joseph back away from Evan. Joseph is in full attack mode and ignores the referee's demands. He begins rapidly clubbing Evan in the back, and does not stop until Evan is face down on the mat.*

Eric: And listen to these fans going nuts for Joseph!

Super Stud: I guess cheaters are popular with these people.

Description of Visual: *Joseph stomps away from Evan, to the center of the ring. To show how fired up he is, he extends his hands and lets out a primal scream.*

Eric: Joseph ready to take it to the next level!

Description of Visual: *Evan rolls out of the ring and tries to collect himself. Joseph is not going to let that happen. He run towards the ropes.*
He sails over the top rope.
He crash lands front first, on top of Evan.

Eric: And Evan taken off his feet, by a suicide dive!

Super Stud: I can't believe how easy a big man is able to fly like that!

Description of Visual: *While Joseph is getting to his feet, the fans continue going insane at his athleticism.*
Joseph turns around. He sees that Jamal is staring at him and moving closer to the action.

Eric: What's this about?

Description of Visual: *Joseph starts moving towards Jamal. He extends his arms in an inviting fashion. He can be heard saying,* "What? You wanna do something?"

Super Stud: This is big mistake! Joseph has the advantage! He needs to stay focused on Evan and not worry about The Jigga-Man!

Description of Visual: *Jamal calmly raises his hands, and motions that he's not looking for any problems.*
Though he is still leery of Jamal and his intentions, Joseph shoos Jamal away and refocuses on Evan.

Eric: Joseph realizing what's import…
…Now what is she doing?

Description of Visual: *Just as Joseph turns around, he sees Cali standing in front of him with her arms folded.*

Super Stud: Now he wouldn't hit a woman would he?

Eric: I'm almost positive he wouldn't.

Description of Visual: *Joseph appears to be conflicted and frustrated. He doesn't want to hit Cali, but he doesn't know how to get her to move either.*

Super Stud: Look at how brave Cali is, Eric! Protecting her friend like that!

Eric: She's interfering in the match, Stud!

Super Stud: She's not interfering. She hasn't laid a hand on anyone.

Description of Visual: *Joseph loudly demands that Cali move out of his way. Cali stands firm, enraging Joseph even more.*

Eric: Oh now I get it.

Super Stud: That's right. It's a trap! Clever girl.

Description of Visual: *As Joseph's frustrations continue to grow, he turns away from Cali and tries to get himself under control.*
Turning away, allows Joseph to see Hagan.
Hagan's plan is thwarted, when Joseph catches his foot as he attempts to side kick him in the jaw.

Eric: Hagan with an unsuccessful attempt at what he calls, the Benally Kick!

Super Stud: Those are some impressive reflexes on Joseph. He's lucky he caught Hagan's foot. A lot of people have been knocked out in the past by that kick!
I mean a lot of people.

Description of Visual: *While Joseph is holding onto Hagan's foot, Hagan tries to maintain his balance. Hagan is also throwing desperate punches at Joseph, hoping that one will connect.*

Eric: Hagan is in trouble!

Super Stud: Yeah and it's about to get worse!

Description of Visual: *Joseph drops Hagan's foot.*
Joseph quickly moves out of the way.
From inside of the ring, Jacob sails over the top, twirls his body and lands on top of Hagan.

Super Stud: How do they do things like that?

Eric: I don't know! But it is completely insane!

Description of Visual: *The fans are really going crazy.*
Jacob gets back to his feet and eats up the ovation.

Eric: We could be on the verge of seeing the Titans get the victory.

Description of Visual: *A chant of* TAU! TAU! TAU! *surrounds the arena.*
The expressions on the faces of Jacob and Joseph change. A look of seriousness has overtaken both of them.

Super Stud: I think, the Soldiers are in trouble.

Description of Visual: *The Titans slowly turn their attentions to Evan.*
Evan is on his knees, trying to use the bottom rope to get back to his feet.
Cali is trying to lend Evan a hand.
The expressions on Jacob and Joseph's faces puts a bit of fear inside of Cali, and she slowly backs away from her friend.

Super Stud: Cali's tough but she's smart too. She knows how to pick her battles.

Description of Visual: *While Jacob climbs back into the ring, Joseph grabs Evan by the pants and muscles him up onto the apron.*

Super Stud: The referee better get some control on this match.

Description of Visual: *The referee tells Jacob that he needs to leave the ring.*
Jacob continues to head to the center of the ring.
Joseph is entering the ring, preparing for his attack.
Evan is still on the mat, but he is crawling to a neutral corner, attempting to give himself a chance to recover.

Super Stud: Evan is a tough guy. But I don't think even *he*, can take on both Titans by himself!

Description of Visual: *After Evan reaches the corner, he grabs the ropes and pulls himself to his feet.*
Joseph is now standing next to Jacob.
The two Titans look at each other.
They slowly look at Evan.
Jacob looks back at his partner and overhand slaps him on the chest.

Eric: Jacob firing Joseph up! We could be about to see this match come to an end.

Description of Visual: *Joseph screams out, "UA UMA!" before charging at Evan.*

Eric: Joseph saying "it's over!" in Samoan.

Description of Visual: *Evan is still in a haze, with his back to the Titans. Evan begins to come around, but not before he gets squashed.*

Eric: And a big splash by Joseph, taking the wind out of Joseph!

Description of Visual: *Joseph grabs Evan by the shoulder, and forces him to turn around.*

Eric: I think this is it!

Description of Visual: *Joseph grabs Evan by the wrist and Irish whips him towards Jacob.*
Evan reaches Jacob.
Jacob quickly hoist Evan up onto his shoulders.

Eric: Look at the strength of Jacob!

Super Stud: Unbelievable, Eric!

Description of Visual: *Evan is laying stomach first across Jacob's shoulders. Jacob falls to the side and drops Evan on his head.*

Eric: Jacob with the Samoan Valley Driver!

Super Stud: That may have knocked Evan out, Eric!

Description of Visual: *Jacob gets back to his feet and points to Joseph.*

Eric: I don't think they're done!

Description of Visual: *The fans are at a full level of excitement now. They know what is about to happen and they can hardly wait to see it.*

Eric: For the fans that have never witnessed this, get ready to be impressed!

Description of Visual: *Joseph turns around and faces the corner.*
He grabs the top rope.
He pulls himself to the middle set of ropes.
In a single vault, Joseph jumps to the top rope.
Then, Joseph back flips off.
Joseph soars through the air.
Then, he lands stomach first onto Evan.

Super Stud: It's insane the way he's able to do that…that…

Eric: Double jump moonsault?

Super Stud: Yeah. That.

Description of Visual: *Joseph covers Evan for the pin attempt.*
Along with everyone else, Joseph expects to hear the referee count the fall.
Unfortunately, Jacob, is still in the ring, celebrating what he believes is he and Joseph's victory.

Super Stud: You and everyone else, may not like this, but the referee is actually doing his job!
The referee has been warning Jacob to leave the ring, since he's not the legal man! He's lucky the referee hasn't disqualified them.

Description of Visual: *Jacob has his hands raised in celebratory fashion, with his back to the pin attempt.*
Surprise and angry overtake Jacob, when he sees the referee in front of him, demanding that he leave the ring.

Eric: I hate to say it but this argument is probably costing the Titans the victory.

Super Stud: Why do you hate to say it? You're actually not wrong,

Description of Visual: *As the argument between Jacob and the referee is going on, Joseph sits up onto his knees. He is confused about what is happening. Hagan sneaks into the ring, just as Joseph is about to get up and investigate. As Jacob makes it to one knee, Hagan delivers a Benally kick, flush into Joseph's jaw.*

Super Stud: Hagan got all of that one!

Eric: Yeah, behind the referee's back!

Description of Visual: *Hagan quickly slides out of the ring, just as the referee and Jacob conclude their debate.*
While Jacob angrily steps out onto the apron, the referee turns around.
The referee sees Joseph lying on his side and Evan still lying on his back. Despite his uncertainty about what has happened, because both men are lying motionless on the mat, the referee has no choice but to begin the standard ten-count.

Super Stud: Now this is interesting development.

Eric: It really is. Will either of these men get back to their feet?

Description of Visual: *The referee's count reaches three, and Evan starts to raise his arms.*

Eric: *Evan now the first one to start moving.*

Description of Visual: *Evan sits up, holding his stomach and his head. He looks around, with a confused expression on his face. As he begins to process what is happening, Evan sees Joseph lying on his back.*

Eric: What's Evan going to do?

Description of Visual: *Evan decides to take advantage of this situation and drapes his arm over Joseph.*

Super Stud: We got a pin!

Description of Visual: *The referee gets into position.*
He slaps the mat once.
He slaps the mat twice.
Jacob realizes that the match is in jeopardy and quickly enters the ring.
Jacob leaps at Evan.
The referee's hand comes down.
Jacob makes contact with Evan's back, but not before the referee's hand hits the mat a third time.

Super Stud: That's it! It's over!

Description of Visual: *The referee signals for the timekeeper to ring the bell, officially bringing this contest to an end.*

Eric: Let's get the official word.

Tony Anderson: Here are your winners: Hagan Benally and Evan Skags, The Sixth Street Soldiers!

Description of Visual: *Hagan and Cali quickly enter the ring, in order to check on their partner.*
They stop as Jacob, who is prepared to defend himself, gets to his knees.

Eric: From the looks of it, this thing may not be over!

Description of Visual: *The referee gets between Jacob, Hagan and Cali, preventing anything physical to happen.*

Eric: You know I have to say that that was an impressive match, Stud.

Super Stud: I expected nothing less from two of the toughest teams in the AWO.

Description of Visual: *Jacob watches as Hagan and Cali start to help Evan get to his feet.*

Eric: Just a reminder everyone, Jack will be out here in a few moments to let us know which of the four women was voted into the final spot of the Modern Marvel Invitational Tournament.

Super Stud: I still think it's going to be Shawntè or Fiona.

Description of Visual: *Jacob keeps his eyes on The Sixth Street Soldiers. As The Soldiers leave the ring, weary from battle, Jacob gets back to his feet. Dejected from what just happened, Jacob places his hands on his hips and lowers his head.*

Eric: This is a tough loss for The Titans. You can just see the disappointment on Jacob's face.

Super Stud: Well then maybe he and Joseph should've won!

Eric: What?

Super Stud: Dwelling on a loss ain't gonna fix anything! Suck it up buttercup and move on! Do better next time!

Eric: Wait a minute, what's going on now?

Description of Visual: *As Jacob looks up, he sees Jamal and Billy climbing up on the apron.*

Eric: I guess they're gonna kick a man while he's down.

Super Stud: You really need to stop thinking the worst when it comes to those two! They have been very well-behaved this evening.

Description of Visual: *Jacob is unsure what to expect. He raises his fist and prepares to defend himself.*

Eric: Jacob saying, if he's going down, he's going down swinging!

Description of Visual: *Jacob beckons for both M.V.T.'s. They stare back at him. Billy frowns at Jacob and hoist his belt onto his shoulder. Jamal is smiling and nodding at Jacob as he holds the belt by his side.*

Eric: This is it I guess.

Description of Visual: *Billy stares a little longer. Jamal continues staring as well.*

To everyone's surprise, Billy drops down off the apron.

Eric: What?

Description of Visual: *Jacob is still not sure what to expect, but he stands by and is ready if Jamal tries to attack.*
Jamal looks at Jacob, still smiling, and shakes his head in a disappointing fashion.

Eric: Wow. Just wow.

Description of Visual: *Jamal hoist his title belt onto his shoulder, and drops to the floor.*

Super Stud: See that? They didn't want any trouble after all. They probably wanted to say something encouraging to Jacob.

Eric: Say something encouraging?

Super Stud: Yeah! You know, something like, "chin up." "Hang in there." "Keep ya head up playboy." Something like that.

Eric: I see.

Description of Visual: *Jacob watches intensely as Jamal and Billy head up the aisle.*
Every step they take, gives Jacob more and more confidence, that the two men are not going to try anything.
As the tension starts to leave Jacob's body, he returns his attention to his partner, who is starting to come around.

Eric: Well as things calm down out here, I'm being told that I need to let everyone know, that Martin "The Intellect", is backstage and is going to be recording some comments.
If there's time, we will hear those comments, before we fade to black.

Super Stud: I wonder what that's about?

Eric: I don't know. All I was told, was that he said he has something to announce for next week and requested that we allow him to make that announcement.

Super Stud: Well at least they told *you* something. I never get told anything!

Description of Visual: *Jacob helps Joseph get back to his feet.*
Despite coming out on the losing end of the match, the fans give them a standing ovation for their efforts.

Eric: You know, despite feeling disappointed, I'm sure this love from the people is helping to ease the pain.

Super Stud: That love is all well and good, but love don't get you to the pay window, daddy!

Eric: Did you really just call me, "daddy?"

Super Stud: Yeah. Back in the day, we use to say it all the time, Jack!

Description of Visual: *The applause continues as Jacob and Joseph exit the ring.*
As they start to head up the aisle, Jack Houston is seen heading down the aisle.

Eric: And once again, the owner of the company is on his way out.

Description of Visual: *When Jack reaches the Titans, he pats both men on the shoulder,*
Jack then shakes hands with the Titans, and commends them for their efforts. .

Super Stud: I'm not trying to tell Jack what to do, but I don't think playing favorites is a smart move.

Eric: I don't think giving a word of encouragement, is playing favorites.

Description of Visual: *While the Titans are heading up the ramp, Jack walks over to the commentators' table.*
He shakes hands with Eric and then Super Stud, and can be heard telling them that they did a great job.

Eric: Thank you, Jack.

Super Stud: Thanks Jack!
Hey, nice suit by the way!

Eric: I never pegged you as a butt-kiss…

Super Stud: Don't! Just don't!

Description of Visual: *A ringside attendant hands Jack a microphone. Jack takes it, and heads to the ring.*

Super Stud: Listen, I don't mean any harm, but Jack needs to hurry up. I got things to do after the show!

Eric: Oh really? Like what? Watch videos of your old matches?

Super Stud: So…so what if I am?

Description of Visual: *After entering the ring, Jack walks to the center of the ring.*
He looks out into the crowd.
A smile appears on his face, before he begins to address the audience.

Jack Houston: Ladies and gentlemen! It is now time to find out who was voted into the Modern Marvel Invitational Tournament.

Description of Visual: *Jack motions to the big screen above the stage.*

Jack Houston: Can we have the winner's name, please?

Description of Visual: *A drum roll is heard throughout the arena, which visibly catches Jack off guard.*

Jack Houston: The suspense is killing me, folks. I didn't expect the drum roll either.

Description of Visual: *Cymbals hit at the conclusion of the drum roll.*
Shock fills the arena when TWO names appear on the screen. Those names are:

"The Real Deal" Brenda Steel
&
Trisha "Chernobyl" Noble

Jack Houston: Well unless that's some sort of mistake, I believe we have a tie. I didn't expect that either.

Description of Visual: *Jack places his hand on his chin and begins to think. Then, he appears to have an idea.*

I think… the only way to settle this, is to have a match next week. "The Real Deal" Brenda Steel will take on Trisha "Chernobyl" Noble. The winner of the match will go on, to the Modern Marvel Tournament and face next week's guest, From the CWF, Bruiser Boyles.

Description of Visual: *A mixed reaction of both cheers and boos erupts throughout the arena.*

Eric: Bruiser Boyles is what they call, polarizing.

Super Stud: From what I've heard, she's another woman you don't want to mess with.

Description of Visual: *As the fans settle down, Jack continues.*

Jack Houston: Now something else that will happen next week, will be a rematch for the AWO World Championship. And I want things between Joey and Dale to be settled.
I don't want anyone to interfere. And I don't want anyone getting away. That's why I've decided, that this match is going to take place…in a Steel Dome.

Description of Visual: *A large eruption of cheers explodes throughout the arena.*

Super Stud: Did he say a steel dome match?

Eric: Yes he did, Stud!

Jack Houston: Now listen, anyone who hasn't seen a Steel Dome Match, they are violent, they are extreme and they are unlike anything you've ever seen!

Description of Visual: *Cheers and excitement continue throughout the arena. The thought of seeing Joey and Dale doing battle in a Steel Dome has everyone ready for the next edition of Big Time Players.*

Super Stud: These people are blood thirsty, Eric!

Eric: Maybe.
But I think it's Dale's blood that they're thirsty for.

Super Stud: Ew. Gross.

Eric: You know what I meant.

Description of Visual: *Jack smiles at the crowd, before continuing his announcements.*

Jack Houston: Now there's one more announcement about next week. And I intentionally saved this announcement for last. And the reason I wanted to make this announcement last, is because of one person… Payne.

Description of Visual: *Boos and jeers fill the arena, at the mention of Payne's name.*

Eric: That man doesn't have a single fan in this arena.

Super Stud: And I don't think the man cares, either.

Description of Visual: *As the audience's verbal disdain dies down, Jack continues.*

Jack Houston: See, despite the way him doing it not being very favorable to me, Payne *did* earn a shot at the AWO New Age Championship.

Super Stud: Yes he did!

Jack Houston: But after his actions earlier tonight, I have to punish him. Now at first, I was going to suspend Payne. But after talking with my good friend, Commissioner O'Mealy, I've decided to have a little fun.

Super Stud: Fun? What does that mean?

Jack Houston: So next week, Payne is going to team up with "The Swiss Aristocrat" Noah Peyrot, and the two of them are going to take on The AWO

New Age Champion, "The Exceptional" Mark Sandal and Sonny Simpson Jr.
But…there's a twist.
If Payne and Noah win, Payne will get his title match in two weeks.
But…if Mark and Sonny win, then *they* will be able to decide when Payne and because he interfered, Noah will get shots at the AWO New Age title.

Description of Visual: *Cheers of intrigue overtake the arena.*

Eric: Seems like everyone likes the sound of that!

Super Stud: Well I don't! It's an unfair decision if you ask me!

Description of Visual: *The cheers turn to jeers when Payne is spotted on the stage.*

Super Stud: Looks like Payne has a problem with Jake's decision too.

Description of Visual: *Payne slowly starts to creep down the aisle, with no emotion displayed on his face.*

Eric: What do you think is going to happen?

Super Stud: I have no idea.

Eric: I'm not gonna lie, I'm a little nervous right now.

Description of Visual: *Payne stops as he reaches the end of the ramp.*
He stares at Jack with an eerie expression on his face.
As he continues staring, Payne tilts his head ominously and smirks at Jack.
Jack is unsure what Payne's intentions are, but he calmly waits in the ring.

Super Stud: Based off of the look on Payne's face, I hope he doesn't do something stupid.

Eric: Well let's not forget, Jack is more than capable of defending himself.

Super Stud: Look Jack is tough, but we all know Payne is unpredictable.

Description of Visual: *With his eyes still locked on Jack, Payne reaches into his pockets.*
As he slowly pulls out his hand, he pulls out a pair of handcuffs.

Eric: Oh my gosh.

Description of Visual: *Payne slides the links over his right hand and takes a step towards the ring.*

Super Stud: Payne, I know you're upset, but this is not a good idea!

Description of Visual: *Payne grabs the middle rope and pulls himself up onto the apron. His eerie eyes stay locked onto Jack, as he waits on one knee.*

Eric: You don't think he's going to attack Jack do you?

Super Stud: Who knows what's in that man's head

Description of Visual: *Payne rises to his feet.*
The tension in the arena is thick, as everyone watches Payne, slowly step between the top and middle rope.
Jack looks at Payne unsure of his intentions. But he's ready to defend himself if he needs to.
Payne is still wearing that sinister smirk. As he stalks over to Jack,. his handcuffed fist is tightly clinched.

Super Stud: This may be what's known as the calm before the storm, Eric.

Eric: You could be right, Stud. And that somewhat scares me.

Description of Visual: *Payne stops and stares at Jack.*
Jack stares back at Payne with a look of uncertainty.
To everyone's surprise, Payne doesn't attack. Instead, he just points to the microphone.

Super Stud: I think he wants the microphone.

Eric: I think you're right.

Description of Visual: *Jack frowns at Payne as he tries to process what's happening.*
A few seconds pass, but it seems like forever as Jack contemplates his decision. Finally, Jack looks at the microphone, before cautiously extending it to Payne.

Super Stud: Not a smart move on Jack's part. Payne's probably going to hit him with that microphone.

Description of Visual: *Payne takes the microphone and puts it to his lips.*

Payne: You're making a big mistake Jack.

Description of Visual: *Surprisingly, Payne looks at Jack, and smiles. Jack gives Payne, a look of confusion.*

Payne: Relax Jack, I'm not here to hurt you. But I am here to ask you a question.

Description of Visual: *Jack continues to stare at Payne.*

Payne: Do you really think this is a good idea? I mean you saw what I did last week to *two* people on my own. I don't need *any* motivation to hurt anyone. In fact Jack, I would do it for free.
But winning the New Age title, and making a ton of people angry, including you, makes it worth it.

Description of Visual: *Payne smirks at the audience.*

Payne: So Jack, you thought that I was going to be upset about this match? No.
I'm actually fine with this.

Description of Visual: *Payne lowers the microphone and looks out at the audience.*

Eric: I wonder what's going through that psychotic head of his?

Super Stud: Psychotic head? There's no need for that, Eric!

Description of Visual: *Payne puts the microphone back to his lips.*

Payne: Just one more thing Jack; what ever happens to Mark…or Sonny…

Description of Visual: *Payne looks at his handcuffed fist and smiles.*

Payne: …is on you.

Description of Visual: *Payne drops the microphone.*
He slowly backs away from Jack, smiling sadistically along the way.

Eric: That man is just pure evil, Stud.

Description of Visual: *Payne steps out onto the apron.*
He looks at Jack.and playfully waves.
While Payne is taunting Jack, the crowd begins to come alive.
We soon see that Mark Sandal is quickly heading down the aisle.

Super Stud: Payne, look out!

Description of Visual: *Mark reaches Payne, and grabs him by the pants.*
Mark then pulls Payne off of the apron.

Eric: It looks like the AWO New Age Champion doesn't want to wait until next week!

Description of Visual: *Mark spins Payne around.*
Payne is unable to react as Mark punches him in the jaw.
Payne staggers away from Mark and tries to get himself together.
Mark stays on Payne and grabs him by the hair.
He pulls Payne backwards and quickly starts striking him in the back of the head.

Eric: And Mark really taking it to Payne!

Super Stud: This is totally uncalled for, Eric!

Eric: Payne interfering in the match earlier was uncalled for, Stud!

Description of Visual: *While our attention is on the fight, Jack as retrieved the microphone and can be and heard making an announcement.*

Jack Houston: I NEED SOME HELP OUT HERE, PLEASE!

Description of Visual: *While Mark is pummeling Payne, "The Swiss Aristocrat" Noah Peyrot, quickly heads down to the ring, with his cane in hand.*

Super Stud: It looks like Noah is going to lend Payne his assistance!

Eric: He's not the only one lending assistance!

Description of Visual: *Noah sneaks up on Mark and is prepared to swing his cane.*
Unbeknownst to Noah, Sonny Simpson Jr. is right behind him.

Super Stud: Noah! Look out!

Description of Visual: *Noah cranks back with his cane.*
As Noah prepares to swing, Sonny is able to grab the cane and snatch it out of Noah's hands.

Eric: Mark and Sonny already showing they can work together!

Description of Visual: *Noah turns around to see what's going on.*
Sonny swings the cane wildly at Noah's head.
Noah ducks out of the way and makes a hasty retreat.

Eric: Noah doesn't seem to want any parts of this battle at the moment!

Super Stud: There's no point in risking an injury this week, if he's gonna compete next week!

Description of Visual: *While Mark is beating on Payne, Sonny uses Noah's own cane to keep him at bay.*

Jack Houston: SECURITY, PLEASE GET OUT HERE!

Super Stud: As much as I love to see a good brawl, where's security?

Eric: I'm not sure what exactly is going on, but I'm being told that security is handling something in the back.
What I do know, is that Mark is really going to town on Payne, and Noah is powerless to stop him!

Description of Visual: *Mark turns Payne around tries to set him up for another attack.*
Payne manages to get his in place, and shoves Mark to the floor.
Payne starts to go after Mark.

Sonny turns around and locks eyes with Payne. This stops Payne from attacking.

Eric: Payne doesn't want any part of Sonny it seems!

Super Stud: The man is wielding a weapon! Would you try to go after him?

Description Visual: *Payne smirks at Sonny as he slowly starts to retreat up the aisle.*
Sonny looks at Payne with a side-eyed glance of uncertainty.
Before another battle can begin, a group of officials and security personnel, start to spill out from the back.

Eric: And finally, help has arrived!

Description of Visual: *The officials and the security team, get between the four men and keep them from fighting.*
Mark still looks like he wants to fight, but Sonny is showing some signs of restraint.
As Sonny lowers Noah's cane, Lord Manny Hayes sneaks up behind him.
Sonny's defenses are down, which allows Lord Manny to snatch the cane away from him and run off to the backstage area.

Super Stud: I see why Noah keeps that guy around.

Eric: Well it seems like we're getting some order restored but what's going to happen next week?
Which team will win a shot at the title? The Sixth Street Soldiers? or Los Intensa Tormenta?
Who will get a spot in the Modern Marvel Invitational Tournament: "The Real Deal" Brenda Steel? or Trisha "Chernobyl" Noble?
And will "The Rock Star" Joey Adams be able to defend his AWO World Championship against "The Natural" Dale Garvin in a Steel Dome match?

Super Stud: Don't forget these four men, Eric? Which of these thrown together teams will win next week? Payne and "The Swiss Aristocrat" Noah Peyrot or The AWO New Age Champion "The Exceptional" Mark Sandal and Sonny Simpson Jr.?

Eric: Be sure to tune in next week to find out the answer to all of these questions!
For Super Stud Marcus Ryan, I'm Eric Wesley. We'll see you next time on, AWO Big Time Players.

Epilogue:

Description of Visual: *The scene we transition to, was recorded moments before the conclusion of the show.*
We are in the backstage area, where we find Martin "The Intellect" standing between the AWO World Tag Team Champions-Billy on his left and Jamal on his right. Martin is dressed in a white suit that matches his clients and a big smile on is plastered on his face.

Martin "The Intellect": I see the red light is on, so I guess that means we're ready.
Ladies and gentlemen, you are probably wondering why I am smiling so hard. Well it is not just because I am proud of the men that I am standing between. It is because the moment that I've been alluding to, will happen *next* week.
That's right everyone! I am ready for my client, to be unveiled. In fact, I've worked it out so that he will be introduced to the world, right before the main event of the evening.
And lets not discount, what I consider the gold standard of the tag team division. I am of course talking about, these men right here.

Description of Visual: *Martin proudly motions to his team.*

Martin "The Intellect": With the training that I am putting them through, as well as the training that they are putting themselves through, it does not matter if it is, the Hispanic duo or the Soldiers from the streets, that are victorious next week. What does matter, is that the M.V.T.'s have the brawn…but most importantly, they have…the brain.

Description of Visual: *Martin points to his head as Billy Foxx begins to speak.*

"Classy" Billy Foxx": You're absolutely right about that, Martin!
There isn't a team here in the AWO, that can compete with us on any level. And it doesn't matter if you're from San Antonio! It doesn't matter if you're from Sixth Street! It doesn't even matter if you're from Samoa! When you get in the ring with…

????: WHAT!

Description of Visual: *Martin, Billy and Jamal look over and see Jacob and Joseph angrily approaching them.*

Jacob Leone: You talkin' about us?

Description of Visual: *Martin slowly backs away.*
Billy puts his hand out, and tries to calm the situation.

"Classy" Billy Foxx: Whoa-whoa-whoa, take it easy big man.

Description of Visual: *Jacob swats away Billy's*

Jacob Leone: Don't tell me to take it easy!
We wanna know if you got a problem with us!

"The Jigga-Man" Jamal Ryans: Yo y'all need to chill cause it ain't even like that!

Description of Visual: *Joseph grabs Jamal by the collar.*

Joseph Seone: Well tell us, what's it like then?

Description of Visual: *Before things escalate, a man dressed in black sunglasses, black leather trench coats, black turtlenecks, black jeans and black boots, enters the scene.*
The man is of African American decent, has an athletic build and appears to be about 6'2 tall.
The gentleman, is carrying a police nightstick and he uses it to hit Joseph in the back of the head.
As Joseph crumbles to the floor, Jacob tries to go after the mysterious attacker.
Before Jacob can defend his partner, a large Caucasian gentleman enters the scene. He appears to be about about 6'4 and has a more buff physique.
The unknown Caucasian gentleman knocks Jacob to the floor with very powerful clothesline.
The two mystery men begin stomping on The Titans, until a team of officials and security personnel run up and and put a stop to the assault.
The unknown men in black don't appear to be willing to listen, until Martin steps in.

Martin "The Intellect": Okay. Okay. Calm down boys. Calm down.

Description of Visual: *The two men stop and look at Martin.*
They adjust the collars of their jackets and calmly start to walk away.

Billy and Jamal are stunned as they look down on The Titans who are writhing in pain.
Martin looks at Jamal and Billy and smiles.

Martin "The Intellect": I told you guys I had protection for you. Now come on, let's go celebrate.

Description of Visual: *The M.V.T's slowly turn and follow Martin and his mysterious associates, leaving security and the officials to tend to The Titans, and The Titans, with their injuries.*

Fade to Black

www.ingramcontent.com/pod-product-compliance
Lightning Source LLC
Chambersburg PA
CBHW051248150726
48001CB00019B/1663